Irene watched Arliss's face, studied her eyes. As Furosa had said, she had made no mistake. She had no doubt that something very dangerous and very beautiful was about to happen.

Arliss reached recklessly across the table and took Irene's hand in hers.

It happened so quickly. One moment they were sitting there, eyes fastened on one another, the next minute they were touching. The room was so quiet that their breath, coming in quick shallow gasps, seemed loud as thunder.

Irene slowly rose and pulled Arliss to her feet. She closed her eyes then and felt her lips touch Arliss's and felt Arliss's hand caress the back of her neck and felt Arliss's body close to hers. Irene disappeared into a world of sensation. Arliss was kissing her now on the face, now on the neck, whispering things into her ear. Irene ran her hands down Arliss's slender arms and caught both her hands. Again they kissed.

Arliss then lifted Irene's hand and placed it beneath her shirt, beneath her bra, against the soft warm flesh of her breast and Irene's knees gave way.

Raging
Mother
Mountain

By Pat Emmerson

The Naiad Press, Inc.
1989

Printed in the United States of America
First Edition
Edited by Katherine V. Forrest
Cover design by Pat Tong and Bonnie Liss
    (Phoenix Graphics)
Typeset by Sandi Stancil

Library of Congress Cataloging-in-Publication Data

Emmerson, Pat, 1945—
    Raging mother mountain.

    I. Title
PS3555.M428R3 1989   813.54   88-29122
ISBN 0-941483-35-5 (pbk.)

About the Author

Pat Emmerson was born in 1945 in the rugged silver-mining town of Kellogg, Idaho, where her father was a preacher. She grew up in Washington and California and moved as an adult to Maine and then to Oregon. Over the years she has worked as a typist, taxi driver, housecleaner, journalist, surveyor, cook, dishwasher, ranch hand, graphic artist, and editor of scientific documents. She currently shares a home on a few acres near Bend, Oregon with one woman, two rats, two dogs, four horses, and six cats. From her dooryard she can see the eastern slope of the High Cascades, where she likes to ride, camp, and hike.

This book is dedicated to Carol, who badgered me until I finished it, and to Dana, Rafer, and Jord, who have not had it easy, but who always had faith in me.

Acknowledgements

Thank you, Katherine V. Forrest and Lauren Wright Douglas, for the superb editing. Thank you, Connie Haring, for doing the first "test drive" on this manuscript. And thank you, Rick, for the word processor and for being the greatest brother a woman could have.

PART ONE
Fall, 1977

Chapter I

Irene Aguilar opened her eyes to the grey light of a mild November dawn in Santa Barbara. She sucked a lungful of air, and the taste of salt filled her mouth. Waves crashed rhythmically onto the sand. Suddenly, the sun burst with crystalline brilliance from behind the mountains and spread itself pinkly across the water.

Along the shore where the ocean swept itself back, sandpipers sank long, needle beaks into the wet sand, while overhead, seagulls hovered and screamed their heads off. Out in the satin pinkness beyond the breakers, pelicans bobbed in graceless harmony.

As the sun rose higher in the sky, Irene rubbed her eyes and pulled herself out of her sleeping bag. She yawned and stretched and stuffed her yellow T-shirt into her stiff, new Levis. The dew had been heavy during the night, so she spread the sleeping bag out over the hood of her rusted blue Volkswagen to dry.

She whistled for her dog, Lou. A moment later the dog bounded happily up, stinking of seaweed, her shaggy coat covered with sand. Irene poured some dry kibble into a paper plate and set it in the sand for the dog to eat.

"Thanks, Mama," Irene said half out loud as she chewed a cold tortilla. "Well, where to, Lou?" she said, a little louder, looking at her dog. The dog wagged its tail slowly. "How's about . . ." Irene unfolded a map of California and spread it out on top of her sleeping bag. With her finger she traced Highway 101. ". . . Paso Robles? You want to go to Paso Robles, Lou?" At the second mention of her name, Lou waged her tail harder. Irene gave her dog a rough pat on the neck.

Irene was elated this second day on the road. The whole world was at her fingertips. Let that dirty, stinking city suffocate in its own brown fumes! From now on there would be no more turning right onto Third, left onto Fletcher, and then swinging sharply into the Spreckles Ice Cream Company parking lot where you'd lock up the old beater wagon and say hi and how's it going to the other drivers headed for their trucks to load up with ice cream and drive ding dong ding dong through the drought-stricken

4

neighborhoods of Los Angeles. She had left behind her a job that was going nowhere, a family that didn't understand her, and a life that was devoid of hope. From this point on, everything — where she chose to go, what she chose to eat, when she chose to stop — was totally up to her.

Irene hummed to herself as she drove north on Highway 101, watching the landscape change from palm trees to scrub oak. Idly, she fumbled with a small portable radio that lay on the passenger seat. She twisted the tuner, scanning the wavelengths. Suddenly a song came through the static — the unmistakable, clear voice of Joan Baez singing Leonard Cohen's beautiful ballad "Suzanne." Irene adjusted the tuner to fully capture the song and the song, for its part, captured Irene.

> Suzanne takes you down
> to her place near the river,
> you can hear the boats go by
> you can stay the night beside her.
> And you know that she's half crazy
> but that's why you want to be there
> and she feeds you tea and oranges
> that come all the way from China . . .

Irene gazed at the road, which she could both see and not see, because Joan Baez had opened her mouth and through this haunting song had swallowed her whole. And in the maw of this song, there stood Irene herself with the mystical Suzanne on the bank of a cool, green river. Suzanne's fingers were long and slender and cool where they touched her lips, cool as they slipped the oranges upon her tongue.

5

The sun set as they stood there, she and Suzanne, as they touched each other — bodies and minds — as they told each other they'd always been lovers. And then they waited together in this magical silence until it grew so dark they couldn't see the water anymore.

Three hours later Irene pulled into Paso Robles — a flat, dry little stucco-and-adobe-clad town embellished by scrub oak and the yellow grasses of late autumn. At the first Quick-Stop she saw, Irene got out of her car and stretched while Lou squatted in an empty lot nearby. The day was warm, the shadows of late fall, long. Irene went inside for a soda and some peanuts.

Near the door, tacked to a well-used bulletin board, there was a small sign, handwritten on an index card: DOUBLE-L STABLE. HORSES TO RENT, $8/HOUR. INDIVIDUALS. GROUPS. LESSONS. The address and phone number were smudged and barely legible. Irene's hand trembled as she fingered the card, as she felt herself actually beginning to shape her own life according to her own dreams. Inside her head, her mother's ghostly voice whispered, "Dogs and horses, horses and dogs. That's all you ever think of. Tell me, Irene, where do you think that will get you here in Los Angeles?"

Borrowing a pencil and scrap of paper, Irene scribbled down the directions the woman behind the counter gave her. She ran from the store, dizzy with excitement, forgetting the soda she had gone in to buy. Seeing herself actually riding a horse for the first time in her life, seized by the power of her

6

freedom, Irene grabbed Suzanne by her mythical arm and yanked her, without asking, toward the Double-L.

The stable was nestled in a small valley that looked sleepy in the off-season. Two large wooden corrals — one holding two saddled horses and the other, empty — flanked a big, unpainted barn. There was a large arena with a low wooden rail opposite the barn and across a dusty parking lot. In front of the barn door a saddled pinto, tied to a hitching rail, stood with one hip cocked.

Irene parked her car in the shade of a huge oak that still clung to its dry leaves. She got out, making sure the windows were left open for her dog. Everywhere was the languid smell of dust and manure. She walked cautiously up to the barn and peered inside. The barn was empty except for thousands of flies that danced a torpid minuet in black, ever-changing clusters.

She spied a woman working behind one of the corrals. She pushed her hands into the pockets of her new jeans, and walked across the dirt yard.

The woman looked up as Irene approached but did not stop working.

"You want a horse?" The woman's green eyes squinted as she grimaced; she was twisting a new piece of wire hard around a fence post. Her blonde hair, long in back, was plastered with sweat where it crossed her forehead. "You'll have to hold on just one sec. I just got a little bit here to finish."

"That's okay," Irene managed to choke out. "You go ahead." Irene stared at the woman's huge forearms as she clipped the excess wire from the post and tossed it into a waste barrel.

The woman straightened up and, with one hand

on her back, wiped the sweat from her face with the other.

"So you want a horse," she repeated now that she had a chance to see her customer.

Irene nodded, although the idea was beginning to seem foolish and embarrassing. She felt so conspicuous in her shoes — her white canvas tennis shoes — while this powerful and experienced horsewoman stood before her in old manure-stained boots.

"I've never been on a horse before. I just wanted to try it," she said apologetically, squinting into the woman's sweat- and dirt-streaked face.

The woman smiled now. "Everybody that rides had to have a first time."

Irene chewed her lip nervously.

The blonde woman thought for a moment, one hand on her chin, and then said, "I'll put you on old Cherokee over there. He's gentle. He's been here practically forever. Just dumb, I guess. But he'll give you a good ride." She laughed and her green eyes sparked in her suntanned face.

Self-consciously, Irene followed the woman to where the saddled pinto was tied to the hitching rail. She stood back and looked at the big horse closely. She examined his big, sleepy face and then, stepping closer, ran her hand down his thick neck and patted him, finally, on his shoulder. He stood up then, and shifting his weight, stamped at the flies that clustered on his belly. Irene jumped back and clutched reflexively at the blonde woman's shirt sleeve.

The woman laughed. "That's just flies. He's trying to get the flies off his belly." Irene face burned with shame.

8

The blonde woman slipped the halter from the horse's head and fastened it around his neck. She took the bridle that hung from the saddle horn and buckled it on, then led the horse by the reins to a clearing where the names of several trails and their mileages were marked with wooden signs. The woman turned to Irene. "Say, if you've never ridden before, why don't you take a lesson instead of trying to do it all by yourself the first time? For a couple bucks more, I could give you a lesson. By the way," she said, "My name's Andrea. Everyone calls me Andy."

"Irene, and everyone calls me Irene."

"Glad to meet you, Irene," Andy said, and extended a dirty, calloused hand.

"I hate to admit this, but I don't even know which side of the horse I'm supposed to get up on," Irene said as they walked toward the arena.

"No big deal. I'll show you. Comes with the package. Where you from, Irene?"

"Los Angeles."

"Downtown?"

Irene nodded.

"God!" Andy exclaimed, shaking her head. "I drove through there once, on the freeway, trucking some horses to San Diego. Thought I'd die."

"Well, I drove through it every day and I thought the same thing," Irene said.

That made the blonde woman chuckle. "Well, Irene from Los Angeles, here's your horse. You stand on this side. It's called the near side in horse talk. Most horses are handled from this side."

Irene took a deep breath and lined herself up beside the horse, praying she was doing it right.

"Take the reins in your left hand. Don't ever get on a horse unless you have hold of the reins."

Irene's hands shook, but she dutifully grasped the reins.

"Now, grab your stirrup with your other hand and turn it so you can get your foot in but not all the way in. You don't want to get hung up in a stirrup. Lot of good cowboys get hurt that way."

Irene shoved off and tried to pull herself into the saddle. To her horror, the saddle began to slip. Her foot still hung in the stirrup, she slumped on her back beneath the horse's belly. With a snort, the horse leaped nimbly aside and Irene felt her foot jerk free. Dazed, the wind knocked out of her, she lay in a dusty heap on the ground, the saddle dangling from the horse's belly.

With one quick motion, Andy yanked something on the saddle and it fell to the ground with a thud.

"You okay?" Andy asked anxiously.

Irene got up, mortified.

"Are you okay?" Andy repeated, touching Irene lightly on the arm.

"Yeah. I just feel pretty stupid."

"Hey," Andy said, and patted Irene on the shoulder. "I'm the one that feels stupid. I knew that cinch was loose. I loosened it myself when I tied Cherokee up. I'm just glad you're okay and not hurt. Here, hold the horse. I'll get the saddle back on." She tossed the saddle pad onto the horse's back and swung the saddle up on top of it. "You sure you're okay?"

"Yeah, I'm sure."

Andy tightened the cinch and took the horse from

Irene, leading him to a mounting block where Irene could get on more easily.

Irene was now terrified. In all her dreams and all her fantasies, she had leaped gracefully onto the horse's back. At one with the horse, she had galloped away across the hills in perfect freedom. But in the reality that confronted her, she was awkward and inept.

The mounting block made it easier for Irene to get into the saddle, and the horse stood perfectly still. She sat for a moment, gripping the reins so hard with her left hand that her knuckles turned white, gripping the saddle horn so hard with her right hand that the tips of her fingers were numb, gripping the horse so hard with her knees that her thighs ached.

"Relax," Andy was saying. "Just relax. I'm going to ask you to let go of the reins for a minute. I'll worry about the horse. You just try to relax."

Slowly Irene loosened her grip.

"Let your legs just hang for a minute, Irene. Take your feet out of the stirrups. That's better. Sit up straight. Just try to get a feel for the horse. Concentrate on how it feels when the horse walks. Move with the horse. Good. Now slip your feet back into the stirrups. I'll place your foot in the right position. You just try to leave it there. That's right. Heel down. Good. Now put your hands up over your head. Move with the horse. Good. How do you feel?"

"Petty good," Irene said weakly.

"Trust me," Andy said. "I won't let anything happen. Just move with the horse. Now put your hands out to the side. Don't draw your leg up. Good. Now I'm going to stop the horse and have you take the reins. Are you ready?"

11

"Yeah, I'm ready," Irene said more strongly, her confidence returning.

Andy positioned the fingers of her left hand correctly around the reins. "You don't have to let go of the saddle horn today, Irene. But technically, you shouldn't hold onto it."

By the end of the hour, Irene was doing figures of eight at a walk and a trot, although it seemed impossible to sit and not bounce when the horse trotted.

"I owe you more than an hour," Andy said, "to make up for what happened.

"That's okay. I've had enough," Irene said.

"You're doing good. With a little practice, you'd be a good rider."

"It's harder than I thought. I'm sore."

"You think you're sore now, wait till tomorrow," Andy said with a laugh. "Why don't you come out tomorrow. I'll give you a free hour."

"I wasn't planning on still being here tomorrow," Irene said.

"Where you headed?"

Irene shrugged. "Up the coast I guess. Big Sur maybe."

"Why don't you come over to my place tonight. Have a beer. We can listen to some music and you can tell me about Los Angeles." She smiled at Irene.

Irene's stomach turned over at the sight of Andy's white teeth in that sunbrowned face. "I guess I could," she stammered, shoving her hands into the back pockets of jeans that felt a lot stiffer and newer than they had this morning. "Where's your house?"

"Over there," Andy pointed. "See that little cabin behind those oaks? That's my place."

12

"What time, about?" Irene asked.

"Make it six."

Irene's hands shook and her head ached as she drove blindly up the stable driveway. She hadn't thought to let Lou out, and the dog whined softly, hanging its head over Irene's shoulder and licking her ear.

"I'm sorry, little dog," Irene said, reaching over her shoulder and patting her. She then pulled over for a moment. As the dog searched for the perfect spot, Irene looked at her watch. Two-thirty. She pulled out her map and studied it. To pass the time she'd drive to the coast, maybe walk along the beach and try to sort things out. Maybe get rid of this headache.

Irene drove along Front Street in Morro Bay and stopped in a parking lot near the pier to stare at the huge rock that loomed from a sand bar in front of her. Fishing boats and sailboats rocked soothingly in the harbor.

But the Embarcadero was crawling with tourists and could offer no solitude, so Irene drove back north to Atascadero State Beach. She pulled Lou's leash out from under the front set and snapped it onto the dog's collar. The tide was out. From the damp sand, Irene could see that big lump of rock rising from the water to the south. She strolled along the shoreline in its direction, hoping the uncluttered beach would unclutter her mind.

Events of the past few weeks came back to her — making the decision to quit work, telling her parents she had quit work, seeing the looks on their faces when she told them she had quit. But she had been justified in quitting! The business had been sold and the new management had announced that all the drivers would be put on straight salary, starting with minimum wage, instead of commission. It meant the difference, in many cases, of a hundred dollars a week! All the drivers, without exception, had quit.

Her mother and father had each been furious for a different reason. Her father had said, "I told you so." He never wanted her to drive an ice cream truck in the first place.

"There's a lot of jobs out there for secretaries," he had said ever since she started high school. "A good secretary is hard to find." Irene could not think of anything she wanted to be less than she wanted to be a secretary.

Her mother was mad because Irene had quit a perfectly good job, even though she was justified. To her mother, women worked at anything they could get until they got married. Then they had their hands full. She herself had taken a job sorting string beans in the cannery until she met Frank.

"Getting a job," her mother had said, "isn't easy." Young people today think all they have to do is walk in there and lo and behold! there laid out on a platter is the world's best, most exciting and highest paid position. If your grandparents had thought that way when they came up from Mexico, just where do you think we would be, your father and I? Life isn't like that . . ."

* * * * *

The sign said twenty-nine miles to Paso Robles. It was five fifteen. Irene, her mind a mess, turned onto Highway 41 and headed east.

14

At precisely six o'clock — Irene made sure she timed this just right — the old battered Volkswagen bumped down the dirt road that led to Andy's cabin. Pulling the visor down against the last rays of the sun, Irene sat for a minute and took several deep, slow breaths. The quiet was broken only by the rustle of a few brittle oak leaves that clung tenuously to the bones of the old trees, and the groaning and scraping of dry limbs against the cabin.

Lou hung her head out the car window after Irene slammed the door. "You stay here," Irene said to her dog — unnecessarily — just to see if her voice would crack. She strode, in spite of trembling knees, toward the cabin.

Andy was waiting for her on the porch. She wore a clean blue workshirt and had changed her jeans. Her blonde hair, still damp from being washed and freshly braided, wet the back of her shirt. She leaned against a post on her porch, sipping beer from a bottle.

"Come on in," Andy said as she thumped Irene on the back. "Have a beer!"

"Thanks," Irene said, not looking at Andy, but gazing around what served as the living room of the tiny, three-room cabin. The walls were rough lumber, fitted tight. A kerosene lantern was mounted above a faded, overstuffed chair. Beside the chair a brick-and-board bookcase held three tiers of paperbacks and a two-foot section of record albums. And beside that, a stereo sat surrounded by a spider's web of speaker wires. An overstuffed couch that did not match the chair was pushed against the opposite wall. To the right, Irene could see a small kitchen with cupboards painted yellow. To the left must be the bedroom.

"So," Andy said as she wiped her mouth with her shirt sleeve, "what made you think you wanted to ride a horse?" She grinned and plopped herself into the overstuffed chair, draping one leg over one arm of it.

"Well," Irene began, but stopped to take a long swallow of her beer, "ever since I was a little kid, I've had this thing about horses. I read *The Black Stallion, My Friend Flicka, Thunderhead, The Son of the Son of the Black Stallion.*

Andy laughed and nodded. "Yeah, I read 'em, too."

"Dogs and horses, horses and dogs. My mother and I fought a lot about it — just the idea of it. She thought it was crazy to even think about dogs and horses when it was plain to see we lived in downtown Los Angeles. My mother is a very practical lady." Irene paused and ran her finger down the condensation that had formed on the outside of her beer bottle. "Well, anyway," she continued after a moment, finally raising her eyes to meet Andy's. Andy was grinning at her, displaying her white teeth and those eyes the color of emeralds. Irene's thoughts left her. She dropped her gaze back quickly to her beer bottle.

"What do you think about riding now?" Andy asked. Have fun?"

"It was . . . harder than I thought it would be. I guess I figured it would come more naturally."

"Oh, it takes a lot of practice. You just have to stick with it," Andy said as she got up and moved toward the stereo. "What do you want to hear?" she asked, kneeling in front of a stack of records.

"What do you have?" Irene answered, squatting down beside her.

"What do you think of Willie Tyson?" Andy asked as she pulled *Full Count* from the stack.

"Don't know," Irene answered. "Never heard of him."

"*Her*. Never heard of *her*." Andy corrected. "I'll put it on. Here, you can look at the album cover."

Irene turned the album over and read the list of songs and shrugged. Then, handing the album back to Andy, she quickly fingered through the rest of the albums before returning to the couch to finish her beer.

"Willie Tyson likes horses, too," Andy said as she drained her bottle. "Saw her in concert once. She said so."

"Then I guess we all have something in common!" Irene said with a little laugh.

"Yeah, I think we do," Andy said without looking at Irene. "I think we all have something in common." She suddenly stood up. "Say, I was going to make us some hamburgers. You're not a vegetarian are you?"

"Me? A vegetarian? No, not me. Not a vegetarian. Not me. I love hamburgers," Irene said, trying not to babble, but hearing herself babble anyway. Her heart hammered away at her ribs. Her palms sweat. She ate half her hamburger, but it tasted like paper.

Willie Tyson sang to herself.

"You were gonna tell me about Los Angeles," Andy said, her mouth full. "Wait, let me put another record on. What do you think of Chris Williamson?"

"Don't know him either."

"He's a her, too." Andy said, chuckling as she slipped the album from its cover. "I'm surprised you never heard of these folks."

Irene shrugged.

"Well, tell me about Los Angeles. How come you left? Where are you going?"

"I left because there wasn't anything left for me there. Where to? I don't know. Just north." Irene pushed the rest of the hamburger around her plate. Andy handed her another beer. "Thanks," Irene said, twisting the cap off the bottle. "How did you get into horses? You always have them?"

"Pretty much," Andy said, leaning forward, her elbows on her knees. "I was in Four-H as a kid. Rodeoed after that."

"Rodeo! You mean like bucking horses?"

"Barrel racing. That's pretty much what there was for girls. Hell! I was the San Luis Obispo County Junior Champion in nineteen sixty-five."

"Oh, do I envy you."

"Well, maybe I envy you, too," Andy said, leaning back into the couch. "You're free. Travelling. Adventure. No obligations. Don't have to get up in the morning at any special time."

"Yeah, but there's money. I have to find work soon or I'll run out of money."

"Ya gotta eat," Andy agreed. "Gets to be a habit."

What else they talked about, Irene, for the life of her, couldn't remember. The air, it seemed, grew steadily hotter and more magical, and time just ran in tiny circles around her. Suddenly she glanced at her watch. It was nearly one o'clock in the morning.

18

"Man! I didn't realize how late it was," Irene exclaimed. "I know you gotta get up early."

"Where were you planning to stay?" Andy asked.

"Earlier I figured I'd probably make it to Big Sur. Now I guess Atascadero State Beach is probably the closest campground." Then Irene suddenly remembered Lou. "Oh, shit!" she said.

"What's wrong?"

"My dog. I forgot about my dog. I need to let my dog out."

"You dummy," Andy said and laughed. "You should have brought her in."

Andy then reached out and ruffled Irene's hair and to Irene the tips of her fingers were charged with electricity. Irene's mind slammed shut and her stomach fell to her feet. She walked unsteadily to her car, Andy following.

"Why don't you just park here for the night," Andy said through the balmy darkness. Irene could barely hear her for the blood that had congested in her ears.

Lou jumped out of the car and ran in happy circles. Irene pulled her sleeping bag out from under the suitcases and turned to go back inside the cabin. The moon, it seemed, so white and full, had swollen until it filled the entire night. She looked at the porch and there was Andy, leaning against a post, her emerald eyes keen, her lips stretched back, her teeth white, and nothing was real. "Bring your dog in," Andy was saying, but her voice sounded so distant.

Irene nodded as Lou padded in beside her. On the living room floor Irene began to unroll her sleeping bag, but her hands were shaking. She felt Andy's eyes on her.

19

Andy knelt beside her. "Irene, why don't you at least bring that thing in here where the bed is," she whispered in her ear.

Irene found herself doing this, but her eyes did not see clearly and her hands did not work right. Her heart was banging away for all it was worth and her throat fell full. Her body was running away from her and she didn't know where it was headed.

Andy turned the lights out. The moon fell whitely across the bed. Irene, stiff in her sleeping bag on the floor, stared hard at the ceiling and saw nothing. Her head was swimming and her heart was too loud. It was jumping up and down on the floorboards and only the sound of Andy's breath overpowered it, filling her ears, filling the room, suffocating her.

Slowly, slowly, Irene turned her head and there saw Andy's calloused hand dangling over the edge of the bed.

Irene floated — she was certain of it, because she could not remember her feet touching the floor — through a hard shaft of moonlight that separated her from Andy's hand. As she wrapped her cold, clammy fingers around Andy's dry ones, a new feeling swelled up in her, growing ever larger, stretching the limits of her skin.

"Come here," Andy whispered.

Irene laid back the covers and before her stretched Andy's strong naked body washed in moonlight.

"My God!" Irene groaned as she lowered herself so that she touched Andy's flesh with the length of her body.

"I was hoping you would do this," Andy was whispering.

They kissed, their lips pressing hard and easy,

brushing lightly over each other's hot skin. Andy caressed Irene's trembling body with work-roughened hands, caressed her loin, held with reverent wonder the two brown breasts that Irene gave her, placed her mouth tenderly between her thighs. And Irene, whose body had not been touched by any but her own two hands, shuddered from the depths of her being.

She lay there in full force of a brilliant moon, holding Andy tightly, and desperately filled herself.

CHAPTER II

The alarm shattered Irene's drugged sleep. Andy stretched to shut it off, then flopped onto her back. She rolled her head to the side and touched Irene's smooth brown cheek with her finger.

"Morning," Andy whispered.

"It talks," Irene laughed softly. "It must be real."

"You talk," Andy said. "You talk in your sleep. Who's Kay?"

"Kay?" Irene bit her lip and looked at Andy sideways. "Just some kid I went to school with."

Andy rolled over on top of Irene and buried her

face in the sleep-tangled hair. "God! you smell good!" They kissed long and gently.

"You've never done this before, have you?" Andy asked quietly. Irene shook her head. Andy pressed her cheek hard against Irene's. "I didn't think so," she said into her ear.

"But I would do it again," Irene whispered.

"Irene, stay with me. I can get you a job here. Even in the winter there's fences to fix and cattle to take care of. Wendell — that's the guy that owns this place — he runs about a thousand head in the hills."

Irene lay silent for a moment, then said, "Andy, you know I don't know anything. I can't even ride."

"Look, half the men Wendell hires don't know anything either. You'll be working with me. You'll pick it up. That's the way everyone learns. Let's have some coffee and go talk to him."

"This is really unbelievable," Irene said softly, smiling a little. "It feels like a dream." She wrapped her arms around Andy's neck and held her close.

Andy parked her old white pickup in the dooryard of Wendell's neatly kept double-wide. She knocked at the front door and when no one answered, walked around back.

Irene got out of the truck to look around. The lawn was parched, and the cheat grass that had invaded it poked foxtails through her tennis shoes. Everywhere was the dry whirring of locusts. She peered inside a shed that smelled of oil. It was packed with strange machine parts: things that looked like giant bicycle chains and things that looked like

23

metal shark's teeth. A spider crawled from between the cracks in the shed wall. Irene backed away. A dog barked from behind a dog house and another sniffed at the back of her legs. She reached down to pat this dog and he wagged his tail slowly.

Andy came around the corner of the house. "That's Grady," she told Irene. "Somebody dumped him at the stable years ago. Wendell didn't have the heart to shoot him. Wendell talks big — you'll see — but he doesn't act big. He's really pretty soft-hearted. He's had Grady around as long as I've known him and Grady's a worthless piece of shit. Not an honest bone in your body, is there, Grade Dog?" She scratched the old hound roughly behind the ears. "Look, Irene. Look at his eyes. Kinda shifty aren't they?" The dog had turned his rump toward Andy so she could scratch him above the tail. Irene laughed.

"Yes, old Grade dog has a criminal mind. He's a fence. See that black dog over there?" Andy pointed to a cow dog that had barked at them from behind his dog house. "That's Joe and he's a thief. Wendell says Grady's his fence. I'm not kidding about Joe being a theif. You leave anything lying around and he'll steal it. Look at all that."

She pointed to a horse brush, two feed dishes, an old sock, a pair of cut-off Levis, a whisk broom, and a cap with the words Let's Rodeo across the front. "He's one hell of a stock dog, though," Andy said.

Andy crooked her arm across Irene's neck and kissed her on the cheek. "Come on. We better go feed the horses. We'll catch Wendell later."

* * * * *

The dismal air felt wet, although it was not raining yet. Irene shivered inside her jacket and hopped from foot to foot on the barn floor. Wendell came in pointing toward the hills.

"Andy, there's four cows out there dropped calves in the last couple of days. Soon's you're through with the horses, get out and take care of them," he said. He was a short man, about sixty, and powerfully built. His eyes, once blue, had faded until they were almost white. Deep wrinkles creased his face from years in the sun and drying wind. He pulled out a pouch of loose tobacco and rolled himself a cigarette.

"We're done feeding," Andy said.

"Number Sixteen again," Wendell said, exhaling and laughing. "Let Irene learn on that one." Wendell walked off still chuckling to himself.

"What do we have to do?" Irene asked, her teeth chattering.

"They all get shots," Andy said around a pencil she held in her teeth. Her hands were already grabbing needles and tags. "We give them a shot of this here stuff that's got selenium in it, and a tetanus shot. Then we stick this tag in their ear. Wendell's got all the cows numbered." She waved a black loose-leaf notebook in the air. "He keeps track of which calves come out of which cows and he knows which bull was in with them. That way he keeps his pedigrees straight. And he knows which cows're his best producers. When beef prices go up, he dumps the bad ones."

Irene nodded and shoved her cold hands deep into the pockets of her jeans — jeans now soft and faded.

Andy tossed everything they'd need into the truck and called for Joe. With the dog in the back, they

25

headed out in Andy's Chevy, bumping and jerking over the pastures.

At the pasture where the cows were supposed to be, Andy let the truck idle and scanned the terrain. "We'll drive up close to those clumps of trees, Irene. In this weather, that's a likely place for them," she said, putting her truck back in gear.

Joe panted with excitement, but stayed in the back of the pickup. A good cow dog, Wendell said, was worth the price of two men. A bad one was hardly worth the bullet it took to get rid of it.

"I see something over there," Irene said, pointing to a clump of oak about a quarter of a mile to the west.

"Well," said Andy. "Tell you what we're gonna do. You drive this rig. I'm gonna get in back. I'll have Joe single out the calf and you drive between it and the cows. Soon's you get upside of it, slam on your brakes. I'll jump out and take care of it. Joe'll hold the other cows off. Some'll kill you soon's they hear their baby bawling. Set your emergency brake, you might have to jump out and help me hold something. Some of these calves are more than a day old and they get pretty strong."

Irene nodded and moved into the driver's seat while Andy climbed into the bed of the truck. Andy gave the dog the command to go. He circled wide, approaching the cows from the back. Rain started — one drop at a time, then more and more. Irene turned on the windshield wipers and leaned over the steering wheel to peer through a single clear spot in the mud the wipers had smeared across the glass. Andy was shouting out there in the rain and waving her arms. Joe was making half-moons around the rear of the cows when one broke from the group. Suddenly Andy was in the back of the truck again, banging on the rear window. Irene opened the truck door and leaned out so she could hear.

"It's Number Sixteen," Andy shouted, licking the rain from her lips. "She's a killer. Took me and Wendell and this other guy four hours to tag her baby last year. She'll ram the truck. Thought I'd better warn you." Andy's denim jacket was soaked and her teeth were chattering.

"What do you want me to do?"

"Don't know yet. We'll try it once like I said."

Irene started off, the truck fish-tailing in the mud. The sky had really opened up and the windshield wipers couldn't keep up. The truck heater didn't work, so Irene, too, shivered.

Number Sixteen lowered her head and pawed the ground while Joe circled behind her. She didn't know whether to watch the dog or the truck or the person. Her baby wandered off. Joe made his move. Andy leaped out. Number Sixteen suddenly made up her mind and went for Andy. Andy managed to scramble back into the pickup bed just in time. Seconds later Number Sixteen knocked a six-inch dent in the side of the truck. Andy lay for a moment on the truck bed holding her stomach and panting. Irene set the brake and climbed into the back with her.

"Wow!" Irene said. "That was too close. Let's try it like this. How about if I drive like before and let Joe separate the calf, but when we get close, I'll jump out and you and I can throw the baby into the back. Mama can just bang away if she wants to."

"Might work," Andy panted. "Go for it."

Irene slid the truck through the mud and once

27

again caught Number Sixteen between Joe and the truck. Irene leaped out and grabbed the tail of the calf. Andy grabbed its front legs and together they heaved the baby into the back and jumped in themselves.

Then Andy went to work. She held two syringes in her mouth, but each time she freed up one of her hands, the calf would nearly get to its feet. Number Sixteen rocked the truck with her incessant banging. Irene had one knee on the calf's neck when suddenly it occurred to her to grab one of the syringes and plunge the needle into the calf's meaty thigh. Pushing the plunger and injecting the medicine was surprisingly easy. Andy looked up, astonished, then nodded and motioned with her eyes for Irene to go ahead and give the other shot, too. Then Irene held the calf down while Andy pierced the calf's ear. In less than five minutes the baby was tossed back out, bawling her head off. As soon as the baby hit the ground, Number Sixteen quit knocking the truck around and trotted off after her calf, shaking her head in still-unvented fury.

"Good work, honey," Andy said, hugging Irene's soaked and frozen body. "It was a little heifer, too. When she grows up we'll have two big, mean mamas to deal with."

Irene wished they were in Andy's cabin with the fire going, having something hot to drink. Her body would not stop shivering, her muscles ached, and her toes were numb. Her tennis shoes squished as she jumped out of the pickup bed to get back in the cab. And there were still three more babies to catch.

"Damn!" Andy exclaimed. "I wish this foolish heater worked." They both hunched over their knees, rubbing their icy fingers. "Well, I guess we might as well get this thing over with."

The next two calves were easy — the offspring of two gentle two-year-olds that mooed softly and watched with dull, expressionless faces while Andy and Irene worked. The last calf was hard to find but Joe finally flushed him out of an oak copse. This one was at least three days old and plenty strong.

Andy and Irene scrambled after the calf, sliding around on the rain-greased dirt. Andy stood for a moment, hands on her hips, breathless. Irene let her arms hang limply at her side, so tired she could hardly move. The dog was circling for what seemed like the hundredth time. Suddenly the calf charged into Andy, knocking her off balance. She was able to grab his tail and he dragged her for twenty feet, filling the waistband of her jeans with mud. Her weight slowed him down enough so Irene could catch up. With the dog at the calf's muzzle, Irene grabbed a foreleg and wrestled him to the ground.

"Shit!" Andy gasped, sprawled in the mud. "No needles." Andy struggled to the calf's neck and held it down while Irene ran to the truck. Irene gave the injections and Andy inserted the ear tag. When they got up they were exhausted. It was five o'clock.

"Let's go feed the horses and go home," Andy sighed.

The hot bath felt more wonderful than Irene could remember.

"Let's eat in town tonight," Andy suggested. "I

don't feel like cooking and I don't imagine you do, either. Besides, you ought to get some boots."

Irene's head rested against the back of the bathtub; her eyes were shut. "This feels so good," she groaned. She opened her eyes then and grinned at Andy. "Know how long I've wanted boots?"

"Well now you need them."

"Where do you want to eat?"

"I don't even care, long's it's hot and someone else fixes it."

Andy and Irene were the only customers in the shoe store.

"Tuesday's not a very big night in town," Irene said, looking around.

Andy picked up a classic pair of boots that were on display. "See these here, Irene? These pointy-toed ones?"

"Those are like Wendell's," Irene said.

"He likes them. I don't. I like the round ones with a regular low heel. I can't walk all day in those pointy ones."

"Wendell does."

"That's left over from his rodeo days. All the boys wore those kind. He's just living in the past. Here. Try these." Andy handed her a pair of work boots.

"Excuse me," Irene said to a skinny kid who was minding the store. "Do you have these in a six medium?"

"Ladies? No. That style don't come in ladies."

"Six men's."

The kid pulled himself up from where he had

been sitting behind the cash register reading a magazine and handed her a box, then went back to his magazine.

Irene pulled the boots on. "These feel real good. They already feel broke in."

"You'll get a lot of use out of those," Andy said as they put the boots back inside the box and walked up to pay for them.

"The first time I fell in love," Irene told Andy one afternoon as they sat in Andy's living room on their day off, "I couldn't think of anything else. All day long I'd sit at my desk with butterflies in my stomach, waiting for recess, hoping I'd see Kay and not knowing what I'd say to her if I did." She chuckled and shook her head, staring at the floor, remembering.

"I couldn't eat, I couldn't sleep. My life was a mess. And the funny thing was, Kay didn't know nothing about it. I was just another kid to her. Just another dumb sixth-grader. I remember when it happened, too. Kay was standing up in front of the class in one of those show and tell things. She was telling the class about how she used to live near Topanga Canyon and she had a horse. That did it. I couldn't believe anyone I knew had ever owned a horse."

Irene got up and walked into the kitchen. "You want some coffee?" she called, pouring herself a cup.

"Yeah, bring me some," Andy answered.

"Oh, I had it bad," Irene continued as she returned with the coffee. "I daydreamed about her.

31

We'd be riding together through these big snow-capped mountains somewhere in Montana, our dogs running along behind the horses. I don't even know if Kay owned a dog." Irene laughed. "The way I pictured it, our horses didn't have to have bits in their mouths. They served us out of love. I don't think we had saddles, either, for the sake of freedom."

Andy laughed.

"Shows you how stupid I was," Irene continued. "You saw how good I could ride when I came here. I'd like to see a dumb kid like me take one of these sour things of Wendell's without a bit or saddle!" Irene gestured toward the stable where the rent horses spent their days.

"Yeah," Andy said. "I'd like to see you take that spoiled thing Wendell picked up at auction the other day. We'd see how much love you had for each other. I'd like to save that sucker for some of the prize dudes we get here every summer. Cocky sons of bitches."

Irene was quiet for a moment, thinking. "Funny how we met," she told Andy. "I don't know what you saw in me. Fresh out of Los Angeles — never away from home before — and you wanted to have me over. I figured you were way out of my class."

"Come on, I want to hear about this woman that came before me." She got up and walked over to Irene, kissed her on the forehead, then went back to flop on the couch and finish her coffee.

"Oh, yes. Kay." She smiled to herself. "I had me and Kay doing everything. Like sometimes I pictured us being veterinarians together, setting up practice in

32

some little dinky Montana town, our lives given to animals, money the farthest thing from our minds. I always had us curing any animal for free if the owner couldn't pay. Isn't that sweet?"

"Real sweet. And just about as practical as your horse training. And it's just a miracle how you managed to cure everything. They just don't make vets like that anymore."

Irene set her coffee down and rubbed her palm across her Levis where the denim had faded and grown thin. "Kay and I always worked in perfect weather. Not this crap you drag me through."

"Montana's different," Andy said. "Sun always shines there, fences don't break, and the cows are sweet and probably tag themselves."

"I know I must have learned something in sixth grade," Irene said, shaking her head and smiling, "but all I remember is being stupid about Kay. And I never even really talked to her. She got sent to a different junior high and I never saw her again."

"Someday I'll tell you about my first love," Andy said, pulling Irene over to her.

"And your second and your third?" Irene teased.

"Let's go for a ride," Andy said. "Let's take a couple of those auction horses and wear them out a little up in the hills."

"I don't want that big bay. He's too rough. I'm not that good yet."

"They're all supposed to be broke. Wendell said they were all rode in the arena at the auction. They just need a little work. But I'll ride whatever one you want in the arena first."

"I want. I'm too young to die."

33

CHAPTER III

The day in May that Gail wandered back into the Double-L was, in every other way, faultless. A late-spring storm had scrubbed the air and polished the trees. The smell of wet dirt diffused into a now-clear, indigo sky. The stable swarmed with customers. Irene was so busy saddling and bridling rent horses that she didn't notice the red-headed woman making her way through the crowd toward Andy.

"Irene," Andy yelled from the corral, "grab Wink

and Bob and I'll get Pecos. Then that's it. We'll have to drive another string in."

Irene turned around and at that instant saw a red-haired woman lay a hand on Andy's arm. She saw Andy jump as thought startled, and something inside of her went hollow.

"Gail!" Andy was saying as Irene came within earshot. "What in hell are you doing here?"

"I came to see you," Irene heard the woman say to Andy. Then quite clearly, "I've missed you."

"I can't talk right now. We're really busy."

Andy was clearly agitated and had not finished with Pecos. Irene took the bridle and pulled it up over Pecos's ears.

"Thanks," Andy said, and took the reins to lead him to a waiting customer."

"Irene," Andy said, motioning her over as Irene started out toward the back pasture where the back-up string was kept. The red-haired woman walked with them. "This is an old friend of mine, Gail Frank. Gail, this is Irene."

They nodded and smiled stiffly and said nothing. The air was tense. Andy dragged her boots through the wet dirt. Finally Andy cleared her throat. "We gotta get these horses. I'll catch you later, Gail." Her eyes, green, so green in the midday sun, darkened and lost their focus.

Irene watched Gail go, then hurried to catch up with Andy. For the rest of the day, she did her work without attention. Her hands caught horses and saddled them and her legs walked them out to the customers. But inside, someone had cut a hole in her belly and emptied everything out.

Try as she would to talk herself out of getting all

worked up, it was like a lecture delivered to an inattentive student. The truth had been written all over Andy's face.

* * * * *

Irene and Andy ate in awful silence, picking at their food, not lifting their eyes from their plates. Suddenly, Irene cried out, "Who is she and why didn't you tell me about her?"

"She . . . I . . . we were together a long time," Andy stammered. "I . . ."

A long silence followed. Then Irene said quietly, "I thought you loved me."

"I do love you, Irene."

"It's not over between you and Gail. It's just so obvious."

Andy pushed her food around with her fork, as if the right words were hidden somewhere on her plate. Her eyes flooded with tears.

"Irene," she said slowly, "I honestly thought it was over. Gail left me, I didn't leave her. I did . . . I do love you." She wiped her eyes with her sleeve, then, pushing aside her still-full plate, lay her head down and let herself weep. Irene pushed back her chair and walked out of the cabin.

Out in the darkness she let herself be sick, let herself sink to the ground, allowed her lips to press into the wet grass. She dug into the mud, and she screamed into the earth where her screams were lost — muffled by the wet dirt and swallowed by the cold night. Lou whined softly beside her, and slowly, exhausted, Irene reached down and stroked the dog.

Toward morning Irene crept into the house and lay down on the couch, but slept only fitfully.

"Where were you last night?" Andy asked Irene, her own eyes swollen and with dark circles beneath them.

"Outside, mostly."

"Irene, we gotta talk."

"It's time to go to work."

"Aren't you even going to eat breakfast?"

"I can't."

During the week that followed, Irene avoided Andy. She slept on the couch in her sleeping bag, rose early, ate what she could force down, and left the house before Andy got up. She could not bring herself to talk. Gail had called the house several times and this evening Andy had met her in town.

Irene turned on some music and paced the floor. Things could not go on like this. In spite of her pain, she would have to talk, and she would have to make plans.

Andy returned late.

"Andy, let's talk now," Irene said. "Tell me about you and Gail and where I come into your life. I get this feeling you were using me on the rebound and it's killing me."

Andy looked at Irene with eyes full of sadness. "Irene, believe me, I didn't use you like that. I honestly believed things were over between me and Gail. I promise you. Believe me."

Andy's eyes searched Irene's face. "Gail and I have known each other since high school," she said quietly. "We rodeoed together — horse-showed against each other. She was the one I went to when I first

37

came out and I was the one she told. One day we woke up and realized we were in love. We lived together for . . ." She looked up at the ceiling, trying to remember, ". . . gosh, it must have been four years. We came to the Double-L together. I couldn't believe it when she told me she met someone else. I just couldn't believe it. She was my life."

"So what made her come back?"

"That's what I was talking to her about tonight. She said she never got over me. She loves me, she said, in a way she doesn't think she'll ever love anyone else." Andy's voice was so soft it was barely audible, and her eyes pleaded for understanding and for pardon.

"I guess that's it, then, for us." Irene spoke to the floor. Andy's silence was her answer. She stood there, frozen, silent, wishing with all her heart that she were somewhere else, or that this were a dream and she would soon wake up.

* * * * *

"Where are you going, Irene?" Andy asked as Irene packed her suitcase.

"First, to the corral to say goodbye to Cherokee. Then north. Oregon, I guess." She tried to keep from crying.

"If you can ever forgive me, write and let me know where you are."

Irene nodded and she turned to head out to the stable just before her eyes filled up.

The old pinto had a special place in Irene's heart. Even after she had learned to ride, she still took the old boy out on occasion, for old-time's sake. His head

38

now drooped in the early morning sun. Irene stood outside the corral for a moment and just looked at him. She climbed through the rails and the horse edged away from her.

"I'm not coming to put you to work, old man. I'm coming to say goodbye." He still eyed her suspiciously, but when he didn't see a halter or bridle hanging from her arm, he returned to his reveries. She patted him on the neck and at the touch of his hide she could no longer hold back her tears and they spilled down her cheeks. She gave the horse a final pat and wiped her eyes with her forearm. Washing her face with water from the stock tank, she dried it with the tail of her shirt. As she looked up she saw Wendell drive by on his way to town and she waved.

She had told Wendell simply that she was moving on. "Sorry to lose you," he had said. "Reckon Andy is too. You ever come back here, come by. And drop us a line now and again."

Andy, she saw, was nowhere in sight, which was a relief. It would save some tension and, perhaps, some tears. She called to her dog and pulled the car door shut. Then, once again, she headed north.

Highway 101 wound beside spectacular ocean cliffs, wooded hills rising to the east. Irene stopped at a viewpoint to peer down at the rocks below, black and noisy with sea lions. She stopped just outside of Big Sur to buy a bottle of wine. Then, following her map, she threaded her way down the tree-shaded roads until she found a campground that was out of the way and nearly empty. She found a tent site that was tucked into one far corner. The nearest neighbor was at least a quarter of a mile away. The evening sky was clear and the day had been hot, so she threw her sleeping bag directly onto the ground, tied her dog to the leg of the picnic table, and ripped the cork from the bottle with her pocket knife.

"Mama," she said out loud. "Papa, look at me now." A long, deep drink and she ached for her home and for the innocence that she had left there. Childhood's end. "To you, Andy," she said, raising the bottle up high and taking another swallow. She hummed softly to herself, "Irene, good niiight, Irene good night. Good night, Irene, Good night, Irene — I'll see you in my dreams." Lavender Jane Loves Women.

Andy, she thought bitterly, would always have a woman around her. She drank again. The trees wove odd patterns in the moonlight. Irene laughed out loud and sang some more, louder and louder, until the tune was destroyed, yet still she shouted and drank some more and grew hoarse until she could only whisper, "Suzanne takes you down to her place by the river," just before she passed out.

PART TWO
Late Fall, 1977

CHAPTER IV

Margaret Mary McGinnis, librarian at the Mobley, Oregon, public library, had been brooding all afternoon over a single blank piece of paper that she held flat upon her desk. Her lips moved almost imperceptibly as she mouthed the words that were going through her head.

"A glance was enough. No more . . ." The words hung there and taunted her because they would not go down on the paper. More words rushed into her head, tumbling and spilling all over one another, and still not a single one would get itself written. A great pile had bunched up until it felt as if her head would burst. Blood pounded behind her eyes.

Suddenly a shadow fell across the paper.

Startled, she sprang from her chair, striking her bony thumbs on the desk in her haste. "My goodness!" she whispered.

Gracie Blunt grinned at her across the Mobley Public Library check-out desk. Her hair was grey as gun metal, her eyes bright as poppy seeds. "I got some books here that's overdue," she said proudly. "That's these here on top." Gracie pointed with her chin to the stack she slowly lowered to the desk. "That's 'cause I read all these twice, they was so good! This one here, this is in Bermuda! This one girl, she was real, real rich but she weren't stuck up or nothing, you could tell that. Well, here she is in Bermuda and this man comes along that she don't know or nothing!" Gracie's ragged head bobbed back and forth in her excitement while her hands scribbled pictures in the overheated library air. "And that's the best one I read this time," she said, nodding conclusively. "But I got these here I want if you don't get mad and not let me take them out with so many overdue." Gracie giggled and shoved the new pile across the worn, lacquered check-out desk.

Margaret slipped her reading glasses on from where they hung from a cord around her neck and stamped the books one by one. If the library served no one else in this rough-sawed town, she thought with a sigh, it served Gracie Blunt well.

Gracie left the hot, dry library with an armload of hope, not due for two more weeks, and walked face-first into a cold November storm.

Margaret straightened things up and got ready to

close. By order of the town council, the library doors were supposed to be locked at exactly five on weekdays. Her glance swept around the darkened room as she pulled on her coat and buttoned it up to her neck. She locked the big oak door and pulled on it twice to make sure the lock caught, then braced herself for the freezing wind.

The wind sliced easily through her coat and drove icy slivers into her cheeks. She squinted to protect her eyes. Although it was only five, darkness was falling and she could hardly see. The library parking lot was a rough scraped-out patch of dirt that had been rained on and muddied up, and was now frozen into a sea of jagged peaks and hard valleys. The walking was treacherous. Margaret stumbled and nearly fell.

The car windshield was a solid sheet of ice. Margaret fumbled for her car key and then had to melt ice from the door lock with her bare hand before she could open the door. Her fingers were numbed by the cold. By the time she had scraped a small hole in the ice on the windshield, they ached terribly.

Margaret, her teeth chattering loudly, turned the key in the ignition and her beloved Ford Falcon, now fourteen years old, the only new car she had ever owned, the saved-for, shopped-for, paid-for car she and Evelyn had bought not long before Evelyn died, groaned and whined and threatened not to start.

With one last protest, the engine finally roared to life and Margaret, clutching the steering wheel with both hands, headed down the familiar route toward home. Her mind drifted back to the middle of Chapter Two where she had left the words piling up behind her eyes when Gracie came in. ". . . the streets shone

brilliantly under the glare of neon lights. The wet
pavement . . ."

* * * * *

Oh Evelyn! Evelyn had known how to live! Evelyn
took each moment between her teeth and chewed
them all to pieces. These moments were, to Evelyn,
treasures to be remembered and enjoyed, but never,
never mourned. Today, today, this is what you have!
she had rejoiced. This she had taught Margaret Mary
McGinnis throughout the years they lived together:
that you are given things only moment by moment,
and moments never return as anything more than
shadows. That you must use each of these precious
moments as they are presented to you, and not be
caught wandering aimlessly off into the distant past
or the unknown future.

The future, Evelyn maintained, is not yet real,
and you can waste too much time there, leaving too
many eggs riding in a too-uncertain basket. And the
past, she said, is no longer real, and wallowing
around in it simply wastes good honest energy on
shadows, merely shadows.

Evelyn's mother, a devout Baptist, had disowned
her irreverent daughter: she was a disgrace, her
mother had said, to a race that was proud of its love
for Jesus. What, Evelyn had asked her mother during
one of their many arguments, was so damn significant
about the suffering of this Christ person when all
around you is the godawful suffering of ordinary
people? Before their eyes, their plain ordinary eyes,
wide with horror at the moment of their suffering, is
spread no Vision of Heaven to soothe them with soft

46

lights and warm promises. And doesn't this, their pointless suffering, their utter helplessness in the face of it, amount to something?

Shouldn't we, asked Evelyn, her black eyes glittering, her black skin tight with fury, be throwing ourselves instead at the feet of all the burned and blistered babies of Nagasaki and ask — no, not ask, beg — beg them for their forgiveness?

And so when Evelyn's heart clamped shut on her quite suddenly in 1965, when she was only 57, Margaret, in spite of her own conventional Catholicism, had had Evelyn cremated and remembered in a small, secular memorial attended only by a few of their colleagues. And Margaret, left so suddenly alone, healthy and alive, had lived ever since in a soft past with her beloved shadow. How ashamed Evelyn would be.

Evelyn's death had ripped a big, ragged hole in her and she had found no way to mend it. How, thought Margaret, can you replace the irreplaceable? She had not even tried.

* * * * *

Margaret Mary McGinnis lay on her bed trying not to listen to the frozen rain pinging against the roof and windows. The storm isolated her from the rest of the world. She pulled the covers up tight around her neck although she was not cold.

The lights had been turned out so the room was black, but Margaret's eyes would not shut. Sleep eluded her. She rolled this way and that but no matter which way she lay, the sound of the cold rain

47

intruded. Finally, she rolled onto her back with a sigh.

If only I could get my mind back on my book, she thought. Earlier, the words had crowded so tightly into her head she had gotten a headache, but now not a single word would come. The story seemed directionless, confused, as though the whole point had been lost. And oh, God! did she miss Evelyn! Death felt terrifyingly close.

Margaret Mary McGinnis reached out with a frail hand and smoothed the cold, empty sheet beside her. She was old. Her skin, it seemed, was wrinkling even as she lay, and there was no way to stop it. In the hidden recesses of her body, her organs were disintegrating, her arteries filling with fat. She felt her liver growing flaccid and her kidneys losing their elasticity. How many times would she have to get up this night to find the bathroom?

Death could come, as it had for Evelyn, at any moment. But Evelyn had not been the least bit afraid to die. She had maintained that death held no surprises. Being dead, she used to say, is exactly the same as enduring all the centuries of silence before your birth. And that hadn't hurt a bit, now, had it?

Besides Evelyn, Margaret reminded herself, some very famous and important people have died. She found it a peculiarly comforting thought.

It would be best, Margaret decided, to go like Evelyn did. Wham! Out of the blue! Like a bolt of lightning, ready or not, there you go. You heart clamps shut, an embolism cuts loose in your pulmonary artery, an aneurism, long silent, lets forth a killing rush of blood, and it's all over. No last horrible moments filled with terror. All the pain would belong to the living.

There had been times, other times, when Margaret had thought that she wanted death to give her plenty of warning so she could prepare for it, so she could capture all the life left in her last conscious moment.

But the most frightening thing of all was that no matter how she chose to die during lonely moments like this night, it would make no difference when the time came. Like everyone else, she would have to take whatever lot was cast upon her.

Margaret clenched her fist and pressed it hard against her breast. The pillow was damp where the tears had rolled from her cheeks.

Margaret threw back the bedclothes and got up to turn on her bedroom light. She went into the kitchen to pour a glass of sherry in the hope that sleep would then come more easily.

* * * * *

Gracie Blunt stretched out on her dirty, narrow bed. The springs squeaked whenever she moved. A fly-specked lamp poured a harsh light directly onto the book she read. Her lips formed the words as her round black eyes leaped across the page.

An orange cat settled itself at the foot of the bed and whipped out its tongue to give itself a bath. Gracie, her eyes still fastened on the page, reached out to the cat with a bare foot and rubbed the animal affectionately. The room was cold and damp, but Gracie hardly noticed, so lost was she in her new book.

Outside the wind tore shingle after shingle from

her sagging roof, but inside Gracie read until late, late into the night.

* * * * *

Arliss Ellis clung to the very edge of the queen-sized bed. Her back was turned so that she faced away from her husband, Howard. He, for his part, tossed restlessly in his place.

Arliss stared into the blackness, not caring that there was nothing to see. She belched and tasted Scotch and garlic from her dinner. Drunk though she was, she could not sleep. Loathing filled her like a pillow, overstuffed, oozing relentlessly into her throat. In the pit of her stomach crouched a secret longing that she refused to name.

* * * * *

Marian Godelski snored soundly with a quilt she and her sister, Gracie, had made pulled up snugly against her ruddy jowls. Around her legs curled two old poodles, milky-eyed and deaf as posts. Beside her, her husband, Herbert, slept as though dead.

Out in the kitchen a big pot caught drips from the ceiling. Herbert would fix the roof someday after the storm. There was no point in worrying about it now when nothing could be done.

A low fire burned in the heating stove and also in a white porcelain cookstove, but the old mildewed farmhouse was so big and drafty that it was still cold inside.

* * * * *

50

Sophie Fortuna sat in a dark corner of Sonny's Tavern. The gloom stunk of stale smoke. Sophie's back rested against the wall, and her legs were crossed at the knee. Her tight white shorts cut deeply into her thighs, and her red blouse, ruffled at the bosom, strained at its buttons. Sophie bounced one leg on top of the other as she peered around the dim room through half-closed eyes. Her lips pursed as though she were in deep thought. She was being ignored and she was bored silly.

Sophie sighed deeply and reached for her gold filigree cigarette case. With a practiced hand she popped open the snap and felt inside with her forefinger. Empty! She slapped the empty case down onto the table with disgust, and, even though it landed right in the wet ring her beer glass had left on the table and she knew it, she left it there.

"Damn!" she swore loudly. She was too goddamn tired, anyway. But now she was mad. She bounced her leg ever harder and searched the dim light for anyone who might stand her for a cigarette.

"Hey John," she called in a sandpaper voice to one of the many backs hunched over the bar. Slowly a figure turned around. "How about a smoke," Sophie said, a smile creeping up one side of her face. The figure sauntered over, two fingers on a pack of Camels stuffed in a shirt pocket. Sophie looked up heavy-lidded at him as he struck a match and held it, cupped against a nonexistent wind, to her cigarette.

"Thanks," Sophie said hoarsely, taking a deep drag and letting the smoke drift up her nostrils. She put her head back and shook her hair.

"Hey," the man said suddenly. "Know what I

heard? I heard there's witches living out on Raging Mother. Eating babies in the woods."

"Get off it!" Sophie scoffed.

"I ain't kidding. Guys I know heard it on the CB. Better watch out for them kids of your'n."

"Let 'em eat 'em!" Sophie said with a coarse laugh. Then, after a pause, "Say, what's your name, case I want to look you up sometime."

"Bill. Bill Hunter. But they all call me Wild Bill."

"Hi, Wild Bill. Pleased to meet you. You a busy fella tonight?" She fingered the snap on his shirt.

He removed her hand. "Damn if you didn't catch me right in the middle of something," he said.

"Shit!"

He strode out of the stale tavern dimness and into the honest blackness of the wet, moonless night. Sophie sat heavily in her chair and dragged slowly on the cigarette. She was irritated and bored to death and there was nothing she could do about it but wait.

CHAPTER V

Arliss Ellis rolled her head back and forth and groaned. She pressed the back of her neck with her fingers where the muscles were tight. The sound of *Sesame Street* drifted in from the family room. A sudden shriek pierced the babble, drowning the noise of the TV.

"Jesse," Arliss screamed, "leave that baby alone!"

Her three-year-old came shuffling into the room, pouting, his eyes on the floor. "I didn't do nothing," he whined.

"Just leave Jerry alone," Arliss said without

turning to face him. "I know what not doing nothing means. Now go on. You'll miss the rest of the show."

When the child had left the room, Arliss sighed and reached for a half-empty bottle of Scotch on the table in front of her. She unscrewed the cap and looked for a long moment at her glass. She thought about getting up for some ice cubes. She shrugged. It didn't seem worth it. She poured the warm whiskey into her glass, then took a long drink of the amber liquid. It seared her throat. Arliss shut her eyes for a moment while the heat of it rose up the back of her nose. She took another long drink and drained the glass, licking her lips while the lingering vapors embraced her like a lover. *Sesame Street* signed off and the two boys were fighting again.

"Shut the damn TV off and go up to your room," Arliss shouted. Just then the front door slammed. It was after five. Arliss's stomach turned to lead. She quickly unscrewed her bottle and poured another drink.

"Join me in a drink?" Arliss asked Howard as she raised her eyes slowly to look at him.

He took off his suit jacket and stared angrily at her with cold, grey eyes.

Arliss's eyes travelled over his body. She hated his neat short hair, the comb marks preserved because he still used hair oil. No one still used hair oil. She hated his white dress shirt, still clean and barely wrinkled. She hated his carefully matched tie that he now loosened as he tossed his jacket across the back of a chair.

"Is that your fourth or fifth?" he asked.

"I offered to fix you a drink," Arliss said through

her teeth. "You don't have to have whiskey. I'll get whatever you want."

"I'll get it myself."

From a room upstairs came the sound of fighting. Arliss drew her lips up at the noise but made no move to stop it.

* * * * *

"Martha, Martha, I love you," Arliss had whispered to the woman stretched out beside her, the morning sun spread like yellow gauze upon her body.

"Did you lock our door?" Martha asked softly. Arliss nodded and giggled into her pillow. It was three in the afternoon and most of the girls who lived in the dorm were still at class, but it never hurt to be careful.

Arliss took Martha in her arms and covered her with kisses. In the ardor of her youth, she made love with Martha, and when they were finished, she held Martha in her arms while they both slept.

* * * * *

Arliss staggered to the stairs and supported herself on the bannister. She called to her sons but they were making too much noise to hear her. She was swaying there, at the foot of the stairs when Howard walked by.

"Get the boys," Arliss said without looking at him. "I'll feed them so I can put them to bed. I can't stand the noise anymore. It makes my head hurt."

"It's not the damn noise that makes your head hurt," Howard said as he went upstairs.

The kids were fed and somehow put to bed. Howard disappeared into his study. Arliss poured herself another drink and stood in front of the picture window. The draperies were drawn back. Through the darkness, her eyes found the street lamp partially obscured by the shade tree in their front yard. Around the lamp was a dim halo caused by the light's reflection on a thick, descending fog. Arliss drank slowly and steadily, staring all the time at that indistinct halo until her eyes could not focus any longer.

At midnight Arliss groped her way to their bedroom. Howard was already in bed, reading. He stared at her from under half-lowered lids. The thick look in his eyes was sickeningly familiar. It had happened before. Always when she was too drunk to do anything about it.

"Don't you," she said through clenched teeth, "touch me." But he did. And he would. This time, next time. Anytime she was stupid with drink. Someday, she vowed as her head spun faster and faster, someday I'll crawl out of this hellhole.

Arliss put her arm across her mouth. Her legs were useless. Her damn eyes were no good. The room spun as she fell hard onto the bed. Then everything went black.

* * * * *

The next morning Arliss awoke alone in the queen-sized bed. The digital clock flashed 10:00 in square, red letters. Howard was at school. The kids were crying in the next room. Her head hurt.

Arliss laid still for a moment while her head

56

pounded. Slowly she reached down to feel the inside of her thigh. A wave of nausea swept over her as she felt something sticky down there.

* * * * *

"Oh, Martha," Arliss had sobbed into the back of her lover's neck. "Why can't we do it? Why does something so beautiful have to be so wrong?"

Martha had no answers, so they just held each other as tightly as they could and cried their eyes out.

* * * * *

The older boy came weeping into his mother's room. He lay his head down on the sheet next to Arliss. Tenderly, she touched his tangled hair. The younger boy wailed away in the next room, trapped in his crib.

"Jesse, honey," Arliss whispered, "go get Jerry out of his crib for Mama, would you darling? And bring a clean diaper. That's a big boy!" The kid wiped his nose on his pajama sleeve. He came back a minute later dragging his little brother by the arm. Arliss pressed her fingers into her temples to quiet the throbbing there.

The baby was old enough to lie down to get his diaper changed, so Arliss propped herself up on one elbow to change him. The pain in her head blinded her. She changed the diaper while Jesse watched with large grey eyes like his father's. Arliss gently pushed the baby off the bed and let her banging head rest for a moment. Then slowly she pulled herself up.

Her blue Levis lay beside the bed where they had been yanked off her the night before. She had slept in her bra and turtleneck. She simply straightened her turtleneck and tucked it into her jeans. She had to pull her belt a notch tighter this day.

It hadn't been like this with Martha. They had loved to eat! Since she had lost — no, not lost, lost was the wrong word. Since she had *thrown Martha away* food had no taste. No texture. There was absolutely nothing appealing about it at all.

She took the younger boy in one arm and went down the stairs, leaving Jesse to bump down on his fanny behind her. She got them some cereal and milk, too sick, herself, to eat.

The dishes were piled up in the sink from last night. While the boys were eating, she ran the dish water. Her head hammered at the inside of her skull. The morning light stabbed her between the eyes. An irritation festered in her chest. And without any control, tears flooded her eyes, and without any control she raised a soapy arm and flung a handful of silverware to the floor.

"There's too damn many spoons," she shouted, and lowered her head to the sink and wept. She saw her boys looking at her with wide, frightened eyes. Big, grey, Howard-eyes.

A voice inside told her to get out of the house, that something was happening in there and it was very dangerous. Hurry, hurry, the voice said. She fumbled with the phone, trying to dial with soapy fingers. Her fingers kept slipping off the dial and she kept forgetting the number. After several tries, she finally got the sitter.

Arliss was sick to her stomach by the time she reached the town library, and the library stunk of sweet wax and varnish. The penetrating odor and the hot, hot air weakened her knees and she staggered backwards into a loaded book cart.

Margaret Mary McGinnis jerked her head up at the noise and emerged from the middle of Chapter Three. Mrs. Ellis looked awful. Her eyes were puffy, her hair disheveled, and her face was grey as death. She stared at Mrs. Ellis just a moment too long.

"Sorry," Arliss stammered, her eyes wild with fright. "It was an accident."

"That's okay," Margaret said quickly. "Why don't you take a look at some of the books on that cart, Mrs. Ellis. There are some new arrivals in that bunch."

"New arrivals," Arliss repeated in a low voice. The words were familiar but she couldn't remember what they meant. She was lost. Utterly lost. A meaningless person in a meaningful world! Could the librarian save her? Did she have a right to ask? Arliss straightened up and placed her hands, palms down, on the check-out desk.

"I'm very sorry. It really *was* an accident," she enunciated. "I'll be more careful next time." Then she rushed from the library.

Outside, the sun boiled in a pot of huge black clouds, and it hurt Arliss's eyes. But the cool fresh air alleviated her nausea and helped her headache. She walked along the sidewalk with heavy, deliberate steps. The hardness of the cement beneath her feet reassured her. Sonny's Tavern, just across the street on the next corner, was off-limits to her, the school principal's wife. Arliss squinted at its red neon sign that blinked day and night. Then she saw Sophie Fortuna who was leaning against the outside wall of Sonny's, smoking a cigarette.

Sophie invited everyone. And Arliss, in her desperation, wanted her. And for that moment — Arliss didn't know how long — she imagined the beauty of embracing a woman once again — any woman — even Sophie. Sophie stared back and flipped Arliss the finger, which jolted Arliss to her senses.

Arliss was overcome with shame. No, she thought with horror. I must not let this happen. I must be a good wife! I must make myself into a good wife. She wiped her nose. I must go home and wax the kitchen floor. That is the perfect place to start. It's a very good thing I sent the boys to the sitter's or they would walk all over it before it gets dry. I will make a nice dinner for everybody while my kitchen floor shines. I will make something special and cut it up into small pieces for the boys the way mothers are supposed to do.

Gracie Blunt passed by Arliss Ellis going the other way and noticed she was weeping, but other people's troubles were not her business.

* * * * *

60

The house was spotless. The boys were bathed and ready for bed. Arliss was nervous and sober. Dinner was strange in its normalcy. Arliss struggled to be polite to Howard from the moment he walked in the door.

As soon as the boys were tucked in and asleep, Arliss crept up behind Howard who was sitting on the living room couch going over the school budget. She put her arms around his neck and whispered something.

The touch of his skin repulsed her. The smell of him terrified her. She hated the stink of his deodorant mixed with perspiration, the hardness of his muscles and the hair that covered the back of his neck. But there was nothing, absolutely nothing she could do about it. Whatever the price, it was what she owed. Whatever it did to her, she had it coming.

CHAPTER VI

Summer, 1977

Furosa Firechild squinted against the sun as she drove into Mobley late in the afternoon this hot day in July. She had with her an inheritance of one hundred thousand dollars in cash stuffed in a ragged stash bag made for her by an ex-lover who had lovingly decorated it with beads and feathers and earthen dyes.

And she had with her a dream.

She dreamed of a village, an Amazon village, built

in the mountains from womunhands. Here, in the shelter of, of, she thought hard for a name . . . Wonderland! . . . wimmin would flock to heal their torn and broken spirits, spirits raped and shredded by a ruthless patriarchy. Here in the bowels of the true mother, the Earth Mother, wimmin could seek refuge and secretly, slowly, surely recapture their power. Wonderland!

Furosa parked her brand new Volkswagen camper — hers now, but surely to belong to Wonderland in the future! To all the wimmin of Wonderland when there were wimmin and there was a Wonderland — parked her camper in front of Pinky McGloughlin's Texaco. She wiped the sweat from her face with her short, fat forearm. Her skirt, hand-woven and embroidered in Mexico, clung sweatily to the back of her thighs as she slid off the front seat. She shook her skirt loose and strode toward Pinky McGloughlin with her arms swinging loosely in the hot, still air.

"Are there any wimmin realtors in town?" she asked the huge red-faced man who stood there watering down the pavement in front of the station office. She raised her arm to shield her eyes from the sun.

Pinky stared at her. Sweat glistened on the hairs in Furosa's armpit. Pinky couldn't keep his eyes from that. All the women he knew — had ever known — shaved their armpits if they weren't too old or too simple or some kind of religious nut. Slowly he lifted his eyes from Furosa's glistening pit to her plump, shaded face. There, sweat rolled from a healthy mustache. A lot of men would be proud to have such a mustache. And on her chin sprouted not one or two hairs like the kind his wife, Esther, had to pluck out every week or two, but a whole fistful. Furosa asked again about wimmin realtors but Pinky couldn't answer. He just stood there blinking his pale eyes and staring at those armpits and letting water dribble from his hose while the sun slowly sank.

"Never mind," Furosa said finally. "Is there a pay phone around?" Her glance swept the gas station lot from one side to the other.

"Yes, ma'am, there is," Pinky finally stammered. "You bet there is. But it ain't here. It's in that tavern you see right across the street." He pointed toward Sonny's and watched, still dumbfounded, as Furosa strode across the street.

Furosa scanned the short realty section in the Mobley phone book and found no womun's name so she shut her eyes and poked the yellow page at random. "North Squahamish Realty," it read, "Darrell McGloughlin, Broker." She copied down the number and the address. Tomorrow she would start her search for Wonderland.

* * * * *

"I got a place you might like," Darrell McGloughlin said, "up on Raging Mother. Pickle boys logged it off here a while back. Some fifty acres, if I'm not wrong."

Raging Mother, Raging Mother! The search had ended. Goddess bless! Wonderland was to be founded on Raging Mother Mountain! Furosa was so ecstatic as she followed the realtor's car those seven miles east of town that her hands shook and she was unable to roll a joint with her free hand and had to go without.

They parked on the side of the highway because a huge barricade had been bulldozed across the only access road.

"Story goes that back about the time of the gold rush," Darrell McGloughlin said, "prospectors that first come into this area found an Injun lady camped in an old hovel up on this mountain. No one else around — just her. Maybe some old trapper's squaw-lady. Supposed to be she had one blue-eyed girl about thirteen and beautiful. Course, them prospectors wanted that beautiful girl. They went up on the mountain, story goes, to take her and I guess that old Injun lady fought them like an old sow bear. I guess she held them all off and got herself and the kid out in the dark of the night. Up and disappeared and took her blue-eyed baby with her. That's the story. Don't know if there's any truth to it at all."

Furosa was entranced. She tramped in her Birkenstocks, huffing and puffing behind big beefy Darrell McGloughlin, up the side of the rain-scarred hill, but it was already her mountain. She had fallen in love. Led by the spirit of the Raging Mother, she didn't see the clay, baked hard as cement, at her feet. Grasping her skirt in her fists, she marched across the violated earth and lifted her eyes above the butchered mountainside, and her gaze swept past the acre upon acre of poison oak that flourished amid the amputated yellow pine and dozer-bruised madrone and charged right over the top of the orphaned fir and came to rest on Wonderland.

* * * * *

"Sold Pickle's place," Darrell told the boys down

65

at Sonny's, laughing and shaking his head like he didn't believe it himself. "Cash, too."

Everybody roared and shook their heads. None of them would've bought it! There weren't one inch of flat land on that piece anywhere. No pasture. No timber. No dirt neither. Just that old red clay. You'd never get a septic permit. Not in a hundred thousand years. No water to speak of, lest you count all of it that dumps old red mud all over the highway every winter.

But Furosa Firechild had bought a dream, an Amazon dream, and it had everything in it.

CHAPTER VII

March, 1978

Furosa sat alone under the eaves of Wonderland's big green army tent and stared dolefully out at the dripping sky. Her chin rested on her hands as she sat cross-legged on her sleeping platform. Twenty other sleeping platforms, all empty now, were lined up in straight rows inside the tent like so many corpses. Furosa sighed, pulled herself up and reached for a shovel and a roll of toilet paper she kept nearby, wrapped in plastic. She shook her head sadly as she remembered the endless discussions the wimmin had had about building a real shitter.

No one could agree on where to put it. Thunderhead and Eagle Feather wanted it right next to the path that led to the river. Others thought it ought to be up the mountain with the front open so there would be a view. They could not reach a consensus. At Wonderland, everything had to be a consensus.

By the time Autumn had convinced all the wimmin that the shitter ought to be up on the hillside, the population of Wonderland had changed, and everyone agreed it was unfair to force those wimmin who came later to abide by a decision reached by their foresisters. Shadows stretched longer and longer and still the shitter was just talk. One by one, the wimmin drifted back to wherever they had come from — San Francisco and Mendocino and as far away as Illinois. Furosa, alone, stayed to dream the Amazon dreams, but she sorely missed having a proper shitter.

Furosa had thought obliquely about building a shitter herself. Two things had stopped her. First, she hadn't the least idea how to start. Second, the sisters who would surely come next summer to make Wonderland their home would accuse her of acting like a landowner. Wonderland, Furosa swore, belonged to all wimmin, everywhere. Next summer, there would just have to be a workshop and a workday devoted to nothing but shitters. That decided, Furosa ducked under the dripping tent flap and headed for the woods.

* * * * *

Furosa Firechild celebrated a gloomy Spring Equinox with Rio de Brazo and Starling from Side Saddle, wimmin's land 150 miles north. Starling said that Side Saddle was having a problem deciding whether to remain "open" in light of the fact that a continually changing population lacked commitment and nothing was getting done about building anything permanent or doing any decent repairs. Also, there was great controversy over Side Saddle's policy requiring all wimmin to change residence every three suns in order to prevent some wimmin, just because they had been there longer or more continuously, from usurping all the "good" places, and also to guard against the insidiousness of monogamous relationships, remnants of the patriarchy.

What had happened, Starling explained, was that Rio de Brazo had fallen in love on her second round of changes and when the next third sun came, was unwilling to move along. Now, it was understood that everyone would move, but Rio de Brazo, in a fit of jealousy, had decided that if she couldn't stay in Far Place with the one she loved, no one could, and to guarantee it she had set about to hatchet Far Place down.

Starling then described, in great detail, the decision ceremony that was held in front of the spectacle Rio de Brazo was busy creating, while she, Starling, wore a decision-maker's mask and offered to take Rio de Brazo away from Side Saddle to heal. Before Falcon could sneak the Answerer's mask past the whistling hatchet and force it over Rio de Brazo's raging head, Rio de Brazo screamed that she could cram it, just cram it.

This negative energy that Rio de Brazo was

creating became so heavy, and began to take up so much space, that the decision ceremony came to an abrupt end and the wimmin of Side Saddle arrived at the quickest consensus in the history of wimmin's land and said yes, take Rio de Brazo away. And the sooner the better.

That, Starling said, was what brought them here to shiver beside Furosa Firechild in an enormous tent and stare out at the rain that had no end.

In the silence that followed, each womun struggled for her own clarity. Rio de Brazo, full of hostile energy, poisoned by jealousy, was unable to find her center at all. Starling felt a name change coming on. And Furosa, sucking fruit drops and absently plucking her beard hairs, fought to bring her Amazon Dream into focus. The Vision seemed hers alone — The Vision she so ardently believed belonged to all womun- consciousness — and The Vision, unshared, dimmed and eroded her power.

A sheet of rain hung from the sky and a river made its way through the middle of the tent, washing sticky red mud over the floor around the sleeping platforms. Suddenly Rio de Brazo sprang to her feet and began furiously to search the tent.

"Toilet paper's in the plastic bag," Furosa offered helpfully.

"Toilet paper! I want a goddamn shovel!" Rio de Brazo grabbed thick handfuls of mud and threw them madly outside, clawing the earth in a frantic effort to scratch a trench around the perimeter of the tent. Little by little the water found the new pathway and agreeably followed it.

"Wow," Furosa breathed. "That was so far out."

70

"It's like knowing when to come in out of the rain," Rio de Brazo said bitterly.

"She's dealing with things," Starling whispered to Furosa.

Furosa nodded and said, "Thank you, Starling."

"River Womun."

"River Womun," Furosa said.

* * * * *

Furosa Firechild sat on her sleeping platform and sipped a smoothie. It had been a month since River Womun had decided, with Furosa's blessing, to return to Side Saddle, and Rio de Brazo, using her old patriarchal name Karen, had left for Michigan devoid of illusion, devoid of hope. Soon, a never-ending stream of wimmin would wind its way into Wonderland from San Francisco and Ann Arbor, from Seattle and Tacoma. This would be the first full season, and every ounce of her womunenergy would be sucked into the all-compelling search for shreds of the Amazon Dream that once had seemed so whole; if she found any, she would be left to puzzle over how in the world they all fit together.

* * * * *

The day of the Summer Solstice Celebration, twenty-seven wimmin from San Francisco, five from Seattle, twelve from Portland, three from Idaho, and a few from odd places no one ever heard of swarmed the green tent and prepared themselves. Among the white wimmin were four blacks and two Chicanas. Furosa was ecstatic.

71

Thundercloud was in charge of applying the body paint. She had brought with her several designs of her own, and several copied from National Geographic.

Furosa called a Circle. She looked around at the fifty or so brilliantly hued wimmin gathered in one powerful ring and her heart swelled and the Dream was clear. Drums she saw, poised beside wimmin ready to play, and recorders she saw held before breathless lips. They were beautiful, these wimmin — these Amazon wimmin — beautiful beyond description. Rattles she saw, decorated with feathers hovering above clenched fists. They were powerful, these wimmin — these Amazon wimmin — powerful beyond description.

Their music began suddenly. At that moment a sob escaped Furosa's constricted throat as altogether this mighty painted circle, baked hard and naked in the summer sun, pulsed and chanted to the beat of one Amazon drum. *Dum-da-da-dum. Ba-dum-diddly-dum.* Furosa saw the Raging Mother herself rise and gather her butchered slopes about her. Then, undulating in a gown of blue and green, Furosa heard the Raging Mother open her lacerated throat and sing her lungs out. Down from the Mountain. Down from the Mountain. *Hey-ye-ye. Hey-ye-ye. Ya! Ya!*

* * * * *

On the morning of June twenty-third, the wimmin of Wonderland began to itch, and the itch would not go away. Tiny blisters grew and spread into lumpy masses of poison all over their arms and faces,

72

between their legs, even inside of their nostrils. Their arms swelled and their eyes would no longer open. The wimmin tried everything — poultices of this and that. Zoriah tried some incantations she had written herself, but nothing brought relief. The throats that had sent songs echoing from the slopes of the Raging Mother now groaned and wept from pure exhaustion.

"Oh goddess of the mountain!" cried Furosa, scratching with the rest of the worshippers, "let me die."

PART THREE
Early Summer, 1978

CHAPTER VIII

The setting sun stained the sky red above the mountains. The temperature lingered in the low nineties as Irene drove past a huge lumber mill on the outskirts of town. Sprinklers kept stacks of logs as tall as houses wet and black.

The sign said WELCOME TO MOBLEY. POP. 760. DRIVE CAREFULLY. She was out of gas and she needed to let her dog out and her head hurt. She had been driving with a hangover through oppressive heat since five o'clock that morning — all the way from Big Sur. She swung into a Texaco station and shut her engine off in front of the pump that read REGULAR. Seventy-three cents a gallon! Every time she filled up, it seemed, prices were higher.

Pinky McGloughlin wiped the sweat from his forehead with one hand and grabbed the nozzle with the other. "Fill her up?" he wheezed.

"Yeah. Where's your restroom?"

"One hell of a hot day," he said. "Not usually so hot this early in the year. It's in back."

Irene splashed cold water over her face and patted it dry with a rough paper towel. She ran her fingers through her hair, tossed two aspirin into her mouth and swallowed them with a drink from the sink spigot. Not quite human, she thought. She pulled her sleeveless shirt out of her jeans and felt a little better for having been out of the car, at least.

"Any camping places around here?" Irene asked Pinky as she handed him a twenty-dollar bill.

He wiped his forehead again and squinted. "No, not really." He paused, thinking. "But you know, you can pull up by the river just about anywheres." He laughed. "Better be careful down around Raging Mother Mountain. S'posed to be some weird stuff going on out there. You never know." He folded the twenty around a wad of other bills and counted out her change.

"Thanks," Irene said, stuffing the change into her pocket. "Where's that place you said now? What mountain?"

"Raging Mother. East of town about seven miles. All talk, ya know. But y'all take it easy."

The sun, it seemed, lingered forever in the motionless sky. Irene drove slowly through town. It smelled of sawdust and pine pitch. Square clapboard houses painted in blues and greens were interspersed between flat-roofed stores and crumbling false-front remnants of the Gold Rush days. Weeds poked through cracks in the gutter and every other corner was an empty lot. On one corner two little boys sorted pop bottles, and from some house window came the sound of a baby crying. A tall thin man sauntered out of Sonny's Tavern, while someone else dragged two small boys past the town library. Three ragged children gathered around a drinking fountain. The biggest one, a girl, boosted the other two up in turn, and when they had all finished drinking, she stuffed something into the fountain and they all ran away.

About four miles out of town Irene turned off the highway and parked beside the river. Lou jumped happily from the car. Feeling dry and tired, Irene threw her sleeping bag down in a small clearing and, in the first half-light of evening, plopped down and stared into the water. She thought: Here's the river, here I am, now where in the devil is Suzanne?

The sun sank and the moon rose like a new quarter floating in a pool of ink. Irene drifted into sleep, coaxed into dreamlessness by the swish of the river, the smell of fish and wet grass, and the caress of a hot wind upon her face.

* * * * *

The morning sun seared the water. Irene peeled an orange and rummaged through her groceries, not remembering what she had put in there to eat. She thought about how hot the day was going to be, and how it was still early in June. She wiped a sticky hand on her Levis.

On the road, a tractor drove by, slowly, bumping along. A short, red-faced farmer wearing a faded denim bill cap smiled at her and she waved back. Something made him slow down, then reach for the key and turn the engine off. He hopped off the seat with unexpected grace.

"Is it okay to be here?" Irene asked.

"Sure," the red-faced man said with a chuckle. "You just stay the night? You going somewhere?"

"I guess I'm on my way somewhere. I'm kind of looking for work and a place to settle down awhile. I just stopped in Mobley to get gas."

The man took off his cap and waved it up and down the road, nodding in agreement. He wiped his face with a dirty bandanna before carefully replacing his cap. "Name's Godelski," he said, extending his hand.

"Irene, Irene Aguilar." She grasped his hand.

"Pleased to meet your acquaintance, Irene," Godelski said, leaning forward and pumping her hand generously. "This here's my place. My hayfields is all on t'other side of the river. I gotta take my tractor all the way around." He laughed. "When I'm rich I'll build me a bridge. Guy I knowed had one field divided up like that. It wasn't hayfield. It was pasture. But he had to drive his cows across a main road to get them out of that pasture. He said the government put the road in after the farm was bought. Ha-ha. Wish I could say they put the river in after I bought my farm. But I can't. I'd just have to say I was fool enough to buy it that way. Ha-ha."

The red-faced man stopped laughing. "What kind of work you looking for?"

"Ranch work, I guess. I worked all winter at a riding stable. They raised beef, too. Down near Paso Robles. That's in California."

"I know where that is. That's down around San Louie. What all'd you do?"

Irene shaded her eyes. "Whatever there was."

"I have a dairy. I need help right now. My boy quit. Well, didn't quit. I had to let him go. But we'll be haying in a month or so. And I got forty head I been doing myself till I could find someone."

"I did milk a couple of the cows out when their calves were sick. I can't say I'm any expert."

"By hand?" He made milking motions in the air.

"Yeah, we put 'em in the squeeze chute and did the best we could."

"This is easy compared to that. These is all machines. Ever do any irrigating? Can you drive a tractor?"

"I can drive a tractor. We had a front-end loader we cleaned out the corrals with. But I never had to irrigate. I was there during the winter and thank God we got some rain this year."

"It was bad up here, too, till this winter. This winter, thank the Lord, we got rain. I never seen hay prices so high as they was last year and I've lived here my whole life." He moved toward his tractor. "Why don't you drop by my house about noon. Plan to have dinner with us. I'll show you what I got and we can talk things over. Half-mile east of here on this same highway. Big white house on the right. Course, it needs painting right now. Says H. Godelski on the mailbox."

81

He hopped back up onto the tractor seat and ground the starter till the engine roared. Then he waved and drove off.

*　*　*　*　*

Godelski talked Pinky McGloughlin into letting Irene rent an old cabin that had been on the McGloughlin land for years.

"I was going to burn that down this year," Pinky told him, "so's the hobos and hippies don't go to squatting in there. Me and my brothers was all going to get out there and try to get rid of some of that brush. That'd make good pasture cleaned up, now we got it logged off." He stared at his shoes.

"But you ain't got anything to pasture on it yet, do you Pinky? And if'n Irene was in there, you wouldn't have to worry about squatters."

"We was thinking about Angus." Pinky licked the sweat from his upper lip.

"You was thinking. But you ain't done it yet. Why don't you let Irene stay in there till you do it," Godelski said, slapping the big man on his back.

"I never did want to worry over a rental. That's why it's stood empty."

"That ain't why, Pinky. Nobody asked you before."

"It needs fixin'. There ain't no bathroom. There ain't no electrical."

"Honestly, Pinky, I believe she'll get along all right. She won't be no trouble. She's a good worker on my place, I swear."

"Well, you tell her to come on by. We'll work

82

something out." The big, red-faced man smiled at this and Godelski nodded his thanks.

After work that day, Irene went into town to see Pinky and find out what kind of deal he would make her. The cabin was old and small and dirty; it needed a new roof. There was no plumbing. An outhouse stood in the back yard and a hand pump brought water up from a fifteen-foot dug well that usually went dry in late August. But it was right down by the river and practically within shouting distance of Godelski's place. Irene squinted until she could see it all fixed up, a small garden planted beside it and her dog asleep on the porch.

CHAPTER IX

Irene woke up at four the morning of the Fourth of July. She had to be out in the hay fields early to finish mowing one field in time to get another one baled before it dried out so much the nutritious seed pods were lost. After this second field was baled, Godelski had said, she could have the rest of the day off to go into town. The parade was supposed to start at ten and after that the Kiwanis had a big country fair all planned with food stands and games and later on, fireworks. The biggest softball game of the year,

Irene was told, always took place on the Fourth when the two biggest mills met head-on at Mobley High.

Irene hopped up on the tractor and pushed the starter. The tractor coughed as she pushed it into gear and lowered the sickle bar. The blades that Irene had stayed late the day before to sharpen cut cleanly through the tall timothy. The sweet smell of the fresh-cut grass filled her nostrils.

As she drove around the field in the first glow of dawn she looked back on the neat swaths she had just laid down, at the clean path the bar she had sharpened herself was silently cutting, and she was filled with pride. She'd like her father to see that. Then he'd believe she could take care of herself. She'd like Andy to see that. Andy would appreciate the beauty of a clean swath. The roar of the tractor drowned the bird songs that Irene knew were just beginning.

The sun flooded the mountain tops as Irene made her last pass around the field. It would be another half hour before its rays would reach the valley floor. Crows screamed their approval as they feasted on pieces of whatever had got caught in the deadly blade. Lou chased terrified field mice that scrambled for cover. Irene cut the last swath and killed the engine to unhook the sickle bar and hook up the baler. She glanced at her watch. It was still early. Fifteen minutes to drive the tractor and baler over to the other field, and two hours' baling would still leave her time to get cleaned up and make the parade.

* * * * *

No one knew for certain who Alta Fortuna's
father was, not even Sophie, really, but there was
plenty of speculation. Now, at eleven, she looked more
all the time like Bill Fergusen, the accountant at
Four Star Lumber. Six-year-old Frankie — he had
something wrong with him — looked a lot like Grant
Foster, the grocer. Gussie was three and there wasn't
any doubt in people's minds that he was Pinky
McGloughlin's. Not even Esther McGloughlin doubted
it.

Alta had made her Fourth of July float all by
herself. She had gotten the idea by herself, she had
found all the pieces by herself, and she had built it
by herself. Her idea was to have a patriotic display —
mostly a costume idea — using a wooden box with
wheels on it. The box would be painted red, white,
and blue, and old metal roller skates that nobody
wanted anymore could be pulled in half and nailed to
the bottom. Alta even knew where such a pair of
skates could be found. Her costume would be a
pillowcase with stars drawn all over it with Magic
Marker, and she would wear a crown made of paper
to make her look like the Statue of Liberty. Gussie
would sit inside the box and hold up a flag. Frankie
would wear a red shirt and blue shorts to match part
of the flag, and he would push the box from behind.
Of course, she'd have to pick out the red and the
blue because Frankie didn't know colors.

The kids were waiting with the rest of the folks
at the elementary school baseball diamond, where the
parade was supposed to start, when Grant Foster
showed up and, disgusted, tried to send them home.
Alta knew she could out-stare Grant Foster, or

anybody else for that matter, and she didn't budge. When the parade started, she was ready.

* * * * *

Virgil Norton passed a rumor around Sonny's that the softball game between Star Plywood and Hadley's Lumber was going to end in a fight. Georgette, his wife, who was secretary at Four Star Lumber, heard in the lunchroom that the boys from Four Star were going to jump in on the side of Star Plywood. White's Mill was going to back Hadley's, and Angie Barczuk told Georgette that she and Ginger would scratch the eyes out of anyone from Star's that dared to walk into the Horseshoe Tavern — they better just stay in Sonny's dump where their kind belonged. So everybody was excited about this year's game and looked forward to it and bought a lot of beer to celebrate.

The parade was supposed to end at the fairgrounds where the Kiwanis had rented out booths. The sun blistered the men who grunted and sweated setting up trash cans. By eleven-thirty the thermometer read 105 and a wilted parade straggled into the fairgrounds. People collapsed in any piece of shade they could find, washed their dusty throats with anything cold, and blew wet hair from their burning faces.

Alta and Frankie and Gussie Fortuna sat on a small patch of brown grass with their tongues hanging out.

"Drink," Gussie whined, clasping and unclasping his filthy hands.

"Shut up," Alta said.

Gussie rubbed his eyes and whimpered. Frankie, who didn't know what was going on anyway, sat quietly in the shade and rocked himself back and forth.

"Stay here," Alta commanded, and sprang to her feet.

With practiced fingers, she quickly removed a leather wallet from the back pocket of a pair of cut-off jeans. Stuffing it under her pillowcase dress, she folded her arms to hide it and walked non-chalantly away. When she thought no one was looking, she pulled the wallet out where she could take a look. There was a twenty-dollar bill inside. Alta quickly slipped the money into Frankie's pocket, and, leaping to her feet, skipped over to a trash can to throw the wallet away. Her hand just reached the edge of the can when she felt something squeeze her arm hard.

"What the hell you throwing away?" Irene yelled.

Alta did not look up but struggled to free herself from an iron grip. Irene shook the kid. "Answer me. I asked you something."

Alta let herself go limp. Then, slowly, she turned around and handed the wallet over. Irene threw the kid's arm down as she opened her wallet and saw that the money was gone.

"Where's the money?"

Irene could see in the kid's angry black eyes that she was thinking about running away. Quickly she grabbed the arm again, harder, and looked around. On a patch of brown grass she thought she saw the answer. Half dragging, half pushing, Irene marched Alta in front of her to where the boys waited.

Irene stared at the two boys. The youngest one wore old yellow-stained underwear, his red-blond hair tangled with bits of brush. Through the tangled mess his scalp showed black with filth. Next to him sat a bewildered kid of about six.

Alta pointed to Frankie, then dug in his pocket and dropped the wadded bill into Irene's hand. Irene replaced the money in her wallet and, not taking her eyes off the kids, carefully put the wallet back in her pocket.

"Where's your mother, kid?" Irene asked and searched Alta's face. A small, delicate chin, stubbornly set, protruded in fury. A mouth, well-shaped, drooped at the corners. Bright black eyes darted from here to there — never looking you full in the face. Half kid, half street criminal.

Alta smiled and shrugged, her fingers spread to show her hands were empty.

"She know where you are?"

Again, the same half smile and empty shrug.

"So what's your name?"

Another shrug. Then a quiet, "Alta Fortuna."

"Wait here, Alta Fortuna. I'll be right back."

In a minute, Irene came back and handed each kid a root beer.

"What's your name, fella?" she asked the older boy, who stared quizzically back at her with crossed eyes.

"He ain't right," Alta answered quickly. "That's Frankie. He's my brother. And that's Gussie, my

89

other brother." She pointed to where Gussie had been sitting, just one moment before, drinking his root beer. She stamped her foot and shoved her fists down toward her sides, sighing with disgust. Then, licking the root beer from her upper lip she said to Irene, "I'll be right back."

"I'll help you look."

They wandered slowly through the languid crowd. They hadn't gone far before Alta spotted him, trailing along behind another little boy, his finger in his mouth and his eyes fastened on a plastic bag of toy cars the boy dangled.

"Gus!" Alta called in a loud whisper and motioned hard for him to come to her. He turned and looked at her, then shook his head.

Irene's eyes fell then upon Arliss and she could not lift them. It was Suzanne, exactly as she had appeared beside the cool, green river, deep in Joan Baez's throat.

"Who is that?" Irene whispered to Alta.

Alta looked at Irene and judged her a simpleton. Everyone knew Mrs. Ellis. "That's Mrs. Ellis. The principal's wife," she explained as though to a very young child. "Don't you even know Mrs. Ellis?" She pointed to the boy Gussie was following. "That's Jesse Ellis." Then she trotted over and grabbed Gussie, who began to scream as she dragged him away. "Shut up," she said and slapped him.

Arliss looked up for the first time. Irene was still staring. Arliss smiled.

Margaret Mary McGinnis strolled by licking an ice cream cone and spoke to Arliss pleasantly, blocking Arliss's view of the mysterious woman. By the time

Margaret had passed by, the woman had turned and was walking away.

The sun had passed its zenith. A breeze stirred and Irene threw back her head to let the sweat dry on her face. The Fortuna kids had tagged along with her all day and she was tired. Alta had filled her in on all the town secrets, all but the one she wanted to know most.

"Who's Mrs. Ellis?" she had asked. "What's her first nam . ?" Alta had screwed up her face, unable to understand why anyone would care.

"She's just the school principal's wife. That's all. Her name is Arliss, and she's always drunk."

"She wasn't drunk today."

"Practically always."

"How do you know?"

"I see her. How come you want to know?"

"She looks familiar, like I've met her before."

Alta shrugged.

The softball game was about to start. It was with great effort that Irene dragged first one foot and then the next up to the middle bleacher.

The stare of the woman with the beautiful brown face had, in that brief moment, burned two holes in Arliss's flesh. A vision of exceeding clarity haunted her: Eyes of the purest black, teeth of utter whiteness. Short, ragged hair pushed carelessly behind one ear, a gold hoop in each earlobe. High cheekbones. Straight nose. Full lips. She reeked of health: her legs well-muscled where they emerged from faded cut-off jeans, her sun-blackened shoulders contrasting starkly against the whiteness of her sleeveless T-shirt. And the vividness of this vision intensified and took on a life of its own and dragged Arliss through the sultry heat of the dusty fairgrounds. So utterly absorbed was she in this, that without realizing it she found herself in the splintered bleachers overlooking the softball field in the waning heat, seated beside Alta Fortuna, her stomach in knots.

On the other side of Alta, Irene sat, and just then leaned back to see who had accidentally kicked her in the back and saw instead the woman of her song staring at her, open-mouthed. Alta bounced up and down on the seat between them. Irene smiled a startled smile and extended her hand.

"Irene Aguilar," she said, lighting for Arliss the dusty bleachers and the heat-drenched air.

Arliss took the strong dry hand in hers and whispered, "Arliss . . ." A long pause followed. She cleared her throat, ". . . Ellis," and gripped the hand too hard and pumped it ridiculously long and felt ashamed.

Jesse Ellis fell asleep straddling the wooden seat and Jerry curled up on her feet. Arliss absently patted one of them and then the other, her eyes turned perfunctorily toward the ballfield.

Virgil Norton was mouthing off even before the game started. Vinney Thomas had jumped one of Star's players and broken his front tooth off. The entire grandstand craned its neck to see who was pitching first. It looked like Star was up and Pinky's little brother, Buddy, was on the mound. The grandstand drew its breath.

The ball came fast for slow-pitch. STRIKE ONE! Bullshit! That wasn't no strike! You blind or something? Damn! There it went again, fast as the devil. Virgil swung. CRACK! It sure connected good! Hard grounder right into center field. Virgil ran like crazy. Red Gillis, Hadley's first-base coach, stuck out his foot and Virgil went flat on his face. "That's for Milo's tooth," he said. Virgil got up with a grimace, his teeth full of dirt. Red just stared. No umpire within twenty miles would have objected. Virgil wiped his mouth and dusted off his pants.

The ball flew wide outside. BALL ONE! Now that's more like it.

The tension in the grandstand mounted. Alta's eyes shone and she bounced up and down with her fingers to her mouth, saying, "Ooooo." There was rumbling and swearing as the balls flew too fast across the plate. Bad calls. Jack Pickle pitched for Star and hit Buddy McGloughlin his first time up. The crowd sucked its teeth in unison.

The bottom half of the fifth and Virgil Norton hit a high fly. Jack Pickle snatched it from the air. Buddy threw one hard and fast and caught Craig Lucchesi in the knee.

The crowd was roaring with one voice and pouring from the stands, fists raised, bottles glinting in the afternoon sun. This is what they had been waiting for. Irene, in a well-timed reflex, grabbed poor simple Frankie by the arm and pulled him to his feet. Leaving Alta to scramble for herself, she picked Gussie up and rushed down the bleacher seats.

The ballfield, littered with broken glass, played host to knuckle-smashed cheekbones and bleeding noses. Curses drifted on currents of air through the

93

evening haze. Sirens screamed in the distance, growing louder and louder.

Irene was out of breath when she finally reached her car. Leaning her head on the door, she suddenly heard someone behind her, gasping for breath. She turned and saw Arliss Ellis, clutching the hands of her two wide-eyed sons.

"Get in," Irene panted. "I'll take you all home." Arliss stuffed her two boys into the back seat. Alta bounced on the crowded seat, laughing. "Ain't you never seen a good fight before?" Gussie sucked a filthy finger.

"All right," Irene said. "Show me where you live."

"You passed it!" Alta giggled.

Arliss reached from her seat in the back to tap Irene on the shoulder.

"Turn left at the next street," she said in a voice that surprised her because it sounded so calm. "I know where they live."

Arliss pointed to a pink and white single wide that stood by itself in a bare lot. Irene stopped by the curb and pulled her seat forward so the kids could squeeze by. Alta smiled and waved as she pulled Frankie and filthy little Gussie toward their home.

Irene then drove Arliss to her house in silence. Arliss leaned forward and said, again in the voice that came too calmly, "Thank you. I guess I should have driven there myself, but I wasn't counting on the fight." She smiled, her eyes on Irene's face, and backed out of the car.

"Oh, that's okay. It's no problem. No problem at all," Irene repeated.

Arliss nodded her head foolishly. "Well, that was

94

pretty presumptuous of me, I mean, to just show up there at your car," she blabbered, still nodding.

"That's okay, really. No problem," Irene said again. The living room curtains opened in the house and a man's face appeared at the window. As Irene's eyes flashed surprise, Arliss glanced over her shoulder. Her face contorted. She slammed the car door and backed down the sidewalk, dragging her two little boys.

* * * * *

The blistering heat wave that had marked the Fourth of July still persisted the day Margaret saw Arliss stagger into the library. Why does she always pick this place? She sighed almost aloud, but smiled as best she could when Arliss's drunken face appeared over the edge of the check-out desk. Suddenly Arliss slid down onto the deeply varnished floor, hitting her chin as she fell. Her eyes rolled inside her head and fluttered beneath their lids.

"Oh! My God!" Margaret cried and looked desperately around the room. Just as she reached for the telephone to call for an ambulance, a moan rose from the floor and Arliss's hand appeared on the check-out desk, and she pulled herself up to a stand.

"Please," she said. "Please take me home."

Margaret glanced quickly at her watch. It was nearly closing. She nodded and patted Arliss's hands.

Pinky McGloughlin was just then crossing the bare library parking lot. Margaret opened the door and called to him. "Mr. McGloughlin, please help. Mrs. Ellis suddenly took sick and needs someone to take her home. Can you help me get her to the car?"

95

"Jesus!" Pinky said. "I know this kind of sick." He took hold of Arliss, draped her over his shoulder and dragged her to Margaret's car.

"Oh, thank you, thank you," Arliss mumbled and leaned her head against the dashboard. Pinky slammed the door, shaking his head in disgust.

"I used to be funny," Arliss said drunkenly. "Everybody liked me. Martha liked me." She turned her unfocused eyes on Margaret, who gripped the steering wheel with both hands. "Was I ever funny in the library, Mizz McGloughlin?"

"McGinnis."

"Mizz 'Ginnis? I'm sorry. Having trouble with my words. Did I ever make you laugh?"

Margaret, confused, stammered, "No, no I don't think you ever did." She reached over and patted her hand comfortingly. It seemed like the right thing to do.

"Didn't think so. And that's why I don't have any friends." Her voice trailed off as her head flopped back against the seat.

"Where is Mr. Ellis?" Margaret asked, hoping he would be home to help her with his sick wife.

"I don't know . . ." Her voice trailed off and a puzzled look came over her face.

CHAPTER X

Irene pushed her shopping cart down the narrow aisle of McEnroe's grocery store. There wasn't much room for one cart, to say anything of two, so when Furosa Firechild came down the aisle the other way, Irene had to squeeze over far to one side.

"Sorry," she said.

"Hey! It's okay." Furosa looked closely at the woman who had just squeezed by her. She was amazed. A third-world working class womun! she thought breathlessly, and found reasons to follow her throughout the store, always making sure their eyes met, always making sure she herself smiled.

Irene was puzzled and curious. Each time they met she smiled back until she almost felt like giggling. This was certainly a peculiar game for grown women to be playing!

The fourth time they did this, Furosa decided she had to say something. She sidled close to her so she could speak in a low, secretive voice. "When you get through," she said as they both opened the milk cooler, "I want to talk to you outside. It's important." Her eyes made a clean sweep of Irene and came to rest again on her face.

Irene nodded slowly and noticed with fascination the beard hairs that stood out so proudly from Furosa's dimpled chin. And then Furosa revealed an unshaved armpit as she reached, unashamed, for a box on the top shelf. Irene finished getting the few things she needed, thinking about those hairs, trying to decide if she ought to meet with this odd woman. What the hell, she thought. I can take care of myself.

Outside the store Furosa tore open a bag of corn chips and held the bag out to Irene before she stuffed a fistful into her own mouth. She then motioned with her head toward a blue and white camper parked on the other side of the street. "Come on over," she said, her mouth full.

"Let me dump these first," Irene said, opening the door of her car. "Get in the back," she said to her dog and put the sack on the passenger seat in front.

Furosa shoved her sack of groceries onto the passenger seat of her van, and then opened the back of the camper for them both. As she pulled her skirt up to step inside Irene saw more of those hairs all over her legs. Unbelievable.

"My name is Furosa Firechild," Furosa said with laughing eyes, her fat little hands wiping the sweat from her dusty face and onto her skirt.

How round and soft her face looked! But the beard. Irene's hand drifted unconsciously up to her own smooth chin.

Furosa watched closely, knowing exactly lwhat she was doing. "You're looking at my beard," she said, rubbing her thumb across it. "It's very precious to me. It's a symbol of my womunhood. It's a symbol that my womunhood lies deep, in here," she pounded on her ample chest, "and in here," she pointed to her head, "and nothing — no hair, no job, no patriarchal pig can take it away from me."

Irene rested her chin on her folded hands and watched in utter fascination. Furosa smiled.

Irene broke the silence. "I'm Irene Aguilar. What —"

"Did I want to see you about?" Furosa finished the sentence for her, licking salt from her fingertips. She chuckled deeply. "You are not like the other wimmin in this town."

Irene flushed. What showed?

Furosa had not meant to cause her embarrassment. She reached across the tiny, fold-out table and patted Irene's calloused hands with her little round ones. "I'm sorry. I'm not making myself at all clear. I live on Raging Mother Mountain. It's wimmin's land. We call it Wonderland. I thought you might like to know about us. You might want to come out and visit."

It was starting to make sense now. Irene smiled

as she thought of Pinky McGloughlin's warning to her the day she had first driven into town.

Furosa continued. "It belongs to all wimmin everywhere, but especially to my Amazon sisters. We're having a celebration of the full moon on Thursday, if you'd like to come out for that."

"How many of you are there?" Irene asked, curious, but not wanting to make any commitments.

"Right now there are about . . ." Furosa pulled at her beard and lifted her eyes to the roof of the van. "I think fifteen wimmin." She whispered names to herself — "Thundercloud, Blackberry, Cedar" — and she counted on her fingers. "They come and go all summer long. It changes."

"Write down the directions. I don't know what's happening that night. Maybe I'll come," Irene said, not half thinking she would, and stood up to go.

"I really hope you do," Furosa said sincerely, placing her hand once again on top of Irene's.

* * * * *

It was the second week in August. Godelski had Irene shut the water off and haul the pipes from the fields to get ready for the second cutting of hay. Irene finished hosing down the milking parlor and, as she watched the debris swirl down the drain, she remembered the scrap of paper Furosa had given her weeks ago with directions to Wonderland on it. She reached in her pocket and touched it.

Irene pulled the little scrap of paper from her pocket and slid into her car. The paper was creased and faded, having been through the wash at least once. She flattened it out on the VW's dashboard and wished that sunset were not approaching. Once the sun went down, it was easy to get lost. One red clay road began to look like any other. Irene bumped across the ruts for what seemed like hours.

The tent was illuminated — a dark mass against the darker hillside. Irene timidly lifted a flap of canvas. The women who were still awake murmured to one another on sleeping platforms lined up dormitory style down the length of the tent. Furosa, alone on hers, sat cross-legged and read in the lantern light.

"Goddess bless," she said, and smiled so warmly that Irene was instantly put at ease. In spite of the late hour and the strangeness that surrounded her, Irene found herself comfortable and unafraid. Furosa's face danced in shadows.

Irene stared in amazement down the length of the tent. So many women.

Furosa smiled and reached for her stash bag and some papers. "Would you like to walk up the path a ways?" she asked, licking the paper. "I can show you around even in the dark."

Irene nodded.

Furosa lit her joint and shut her eyes as she inhaled deeply. "Hit?"

Irene shook her head. Furosa exhaled slowly. "Don't smoke?"

Irene shook her head.

They walked in silence for some time and then Furosa began to tell her about Wonderland and the hope she held for it.

Irene listened. Then, in the intimacy of darkness, she began to talk.

"Have you ever fallen in love with a song?" she asked her strange companion.

"Yes," Furosa said, yes she had. She had fallen in love with songs, while songs played, and through songs — even while singing songs. "Music," Furosa said, "is a great facilitator of love. It is an act of creation and an act of communication on one of the very deepest levels."

"I fell in love," Irene said, "with this vision that came out of this one particular song. And then — I know this sounds stupid — I met this woman and she was exactly like I saw her in this song. It's really spooky."

"Goddess bless," Furosa said. "A sister is calling to you and I think you have a responsibility to answer that call."

"One small problem," Irene said. "She's married. She's even got two little kids."

"Big fucking deal. Irene, there are all kinds of love and all kinds of calls. Listen to what *this* womun wants," Furosa said. "Listen to *her*."

They talked into the wee hours of the morning. Irene, yawning, said, "I've got to go home. I've got to be at work in an hour and a half."

"I'm so glad you came by," Furosa said. "There aren't a lot of dykes in a town like Mobley and I figures you'd be pretty lonesome."

Irene was shocked into silence. Furosa, seeing this, turned toward her and mouthed the word "lesbian" and then "dyke." Then she whispered, keeping her voice low to avoid disturbing the sleeping wimmin, "Lesbian, lesbian, lesbian. Go on. Say it. Dyke, dyke, dyke. Let me hear you say it."

But the words stuck in Irene's throat. Even

conceiving of them was hard. They sounded so dirty, whereas the things she had done, the love she had felt seemed so pure and clean.

"Take the words they sling at you and make them yours," Furosa urgently whispered. "Cherish them. Embrace them. Don't allow those who have no appreciation for them to sully them in front of you. Say it! Come on, say it with me! Lezzzbian. Say dyke, Irene! Say it! They're your words, for goddess sake!"

But Irene's lips were stuck shut. And it was time to go to work.

* * * * *

Irene took a deep breath and finally allowed herself to finish dialing the phone. Her heart pounded while it rang.

"Irene Aguilar. I gave you a ride home when that fight broke out at the softball game." There was a long silence, long enough for Irene to wonder if she had made a mistake.

"Yes," came a weak answer. "Yes, I remember."

"I'm calling to . . . ah . . . to see if maybe you wanted to bring your kids out here where I live and have a picnic down by the river. I was going to run into town and see if I can find my little friends, the Fortuna kids. To see if they can come." There it was, all out. She had said it. If Arliss turned her down it would be a relief.

"I, well, I guess," Arliss stammered. Then she took a deep breath herself, looking firmly at the clock on her kitchen wall, and answered in a loud voice that was terrifyingly calm, "That sounds wonderful. What time and give me directions."

103

As she described the turnoff, Irene hoped she was making sense but wasn't at all sure.

"What can I bring?" Arliss asked.

"Bring whatever you want. I'll have stuff, too. It doesn't really matter," Irene said, her heart now beating hard with excitement.

Irene found the Fortuna kids coming out of McEnroe's store where they had just turned in a bunch of pop bottles. Twice now she had taken all three of the kids somewhere. To the Dairy Queen and for carnival rides set up in a shopping mall parking lot. Their mother hardly knew where they were or what they were doing so it was usually up to Alta. Every once in a while, Alta told Irene, Sophie would throw her across the room, but it never had anything to do with where they had all been or what they had been doing. Sophie never laid a hand on Frankie, either to love him or to hate him. And Gussie was her favorite. That meant she held him sometimes and kissed his forehead. But she didn't care where Alta took them or what they did when she took them there.

Alta was excited about a picnic and chattered nonstop while she skipped along behind Irene, helping her to pick out potato chips and Kool-Aid and bologna for their sandwiches. With exaggerated motherliness, she took Frankie by the hand and guided him into the back seat of Irene's car. She pushed Gussie roughly in beside him, then seated herself in the front and bounced on the seat beside Irene and sang at the top of her lungs.

* * * * *

104

Arliss was afraid she was lost. She pulled over and read her directions for the third time. Although she was going the way the directions said, it didn't look as if anyone lived nearby, so she turned around and backtracked for the second time. Her patience was exhausted and her boys were screaming at each other over a string of red licorice when she finally pulled into the clearing behind Irene's cabin.

Irene watched Arliss shut the car door. Arliss came walking toward her, wearing a pair of faded cut-off jeans that were too big and bunched up around her waist where she had drawn the belt tight. A red and white striped shirt, the sleeves rolled up, had been hastily tucked into the cut-offs. Her auburn hair was caught at the nape of her neck and the sun on it made it glisten. In one arm she carried a large grocery sack, and she dragged her youngest boy with the other. She was Suzanne in the sunlight on a hot summer day.

"Hi," Irene said. "I was just going to teach this kid to swim." Irene nodded toward Alta who was standing up to her knees in the river with her arms clutching her own shoulders, shivering. Irene's dog ran frantically up and down the shore. Lou, hating water as much as she did, worried herself silly when people went in .

Arliss let go of her kid and set the grocery bag down on the blanket, dragging the food out item by item. "I brought a few things. I hope you like them. These little things — kiwi fruit — I like them. The kids hate them. But they just like bananas. And I brought these good crackers and some nice, ripe Brie. It's hard to find good Brie here."

Irene laughed and threw herself backwards onto her blanket. Wow. Oh wow, she thought. Next it'll be tea and oranges.

"You don't like them, either?"

Irene was still laughing. "I've never tried them. But I will try them." Then she turned over and, resting her chin on her hand said, "My family never bought stuff like that."

"Irene," Alta called from the water, her teeth chattering, "hurry."

Irene sprang to her feet and waded into the river. Together Alta and Irene pushed their way out into the current where the late summer water reached Alta's waist.

One person in the water was bad enough on Lou's nerves, but two set her to yapping. "I'm going to tie her up by the house," Irene said to Alta. "She's going to drive me nuts. Be back in a sec."

Irene waded out of the water. "Do you mind watching the kid for a minute?" she asked Arliss. "I've got to get rid of this stupid dog."

Arliss shook her head and smiled. Her boys were fighting with Gussie over a toy. Frankie sat underneath a tree and rocked himself. Arliss stood on the shore and watched, her arms crossed, thinking, and she allowed herself, for the first time in years, to feel at peace. She closed her eyes for a moment and listened to the river — took a deep breath and smelled its dampness. A hot breeze hugged her with soft summer arms and she let it.

Irene was trotting across the grass on her way to the river. Arliss watched as Irene scrambled down the bank and waded across to where the ragged child shivered, watched as Irene took Alta's head in her hands and helped the kid to float on her back.

Irene came out of the water laughing and shaking the water from her hands. "Did you see her do it?" she asked Arliss, pointing to Alta, who stood beside her shaking as much from excitement as from the cold.

Arliss put her hand gently on Alta's hair and pushed her head back so that she could look Alta straight in the face. "Alta, that was really good," and the tears that threatened had nothing to do with the kid.

Irene mixed Kool Aid and gave Alta a bag of potato chips for the kids to share while Arliss threw together some bologna sandwiches for them.

"What you don't use out of that package," Irene said, "I'll give to my dog. I don't have a real refrigerator."

"What do you use?"

"I hang a bag down the well. Keeps most things cool, but I wouldn't trust meat down there very long. Mostly I don't buy anything that really has to be kept cold."

Arliss cut a piece of cheese from the pie-shaped wedge that was beginning to melt in the August heat. She spread this out onto a whole-wheat cracker and handed it to Irene, smiling.

"Do you eat this white stuff?" Irene asked, pointing to the moldy rind.

"That's the best part."

Irene smelled it carefully before putting it to her lips and taking the tiniest of bites. She chewed slowly. "Not bad," she said, nodding.

107

"More?"

"I think I'll have the next one with bologna."

After they ate, Irene took the kids to show them where she had found an arrowhead. The spot was nearby so Irene left the kids there looking for more. Arliss's youngest boy stayed with the other three, even though he was too young to have the foggiest notion what they were doing. Arliss watched, again fascinated by Irene's patience and interest. Her own life, it seemed, was so absorbed by its turmoil that outside interests had escaped her. She had forgotten people had them.

Irene gave Alta another swimming lesson and this time the kid floated face down holding her breath. The current was too swift for the little boys, so Irene made them a small "pool" out of rocks. They played hard as the sun dropped lower and lower in the sky.

Alta was exhausted and went up to Irene's cabin to lie down. The boys lay down on the grass and soon fell asleep. Arliss and Irene sat on the blanket and watched the river.

"I really want to thank you for inviting me out here," Arliss said softly, not wanting to disturb the peace that surrounded her. I . . ." She hesitated, swallowed, then reached for a kiwi fruit to cut for both of them. "I . . ." she began again, "don't know when I've felt so good." She looked up into Irene's gentle face and allowed her eyes to rest there for a moment.

Irene, leaning back on her elbows, looked back into the face of Suzanne and felt the evening creep upon them, listened to the river, listened to her song. It was more perfect than her dreams. "Me either," Irene whispered.

The balmy summer wind, it seemed, blew through them and caressed them from the inside out. Arliss, in the beauty of the moment, nearly touched Irene, nearly ran her fingers down Irene's sun-darkened forearm, nearly let them come to rest on top of Irene's strong hand.

Irene's heart was trying to force its way out her throat. She swallowed hard and with all the strength she could muster, pulled her gaze from the face of her dream and forced it onto the ever-darkening river. But the heat of the woman beside her tormented her flesh.

"I'll try some more of your cheese," Irene said, clearing her throat and reaching for the now-liquid cheese. Arliss smiled and edged it to her. "Just stick your finger in the middle," Arliss said.

"Not bad," Irene said, licking her finger. "I've never had anything like it before. I like those little dealies, too. What did you call them? Kiwi fruit?"

"You can't always find them in the stores," Arliss said, wrapping the cheese up to protect it from the flies.

"Do you want to walk up the river a bit?" Irene asked in a voice that she was sure came out too loud and too harsh. She had to move, had to get up to keep herself from touching this woman and regretting it later.

Arliss glanced at the sleeping boys.

"I think they're dead," Irene said.

"I'm going to have to go soon," Arliss said.

"I guess I better, too. I gotta take Alta and them back."

"I can drop them off for you," Arliss offered.

"That's okay, I've got to do a couple of errands anyway."

Irene got up and dusted off the still-damp back of her shorts. Arliss, hands in her pockets, ambled beside her. Irene listened to the water, listened to the sounds of twilight — the crickets and the bullbats and the downslope wind sliding off the mountains.

"Irene," Arliss said finally. "Thank you. This whole day has been absolutely beautiful."

Irene turned toward her and smiled.

"It was for me, too." She paused for a moment and looked down as she kicked some dirt around. Then she raised her eyes again to Arliss's face. "Do you want to get together again? Maybe have dinner and see a movie?"

"I'd like that," Arliss said as she rubbed some mosquitoes off her arms. "I better get back and check on the boys. The mosquitoes will be getting to them, too."

They walked back in silence. Irene helped Arliss carry her sleeping boys to the car.

"I'll call you Wednesday," Irene said. "I don't have a phone out here so you can't call me."

"Call before five," Arliss said.

Irene felt as if she were floating as she watched the taillights of Arliss's car disappear into the violet evening. She loaded up the Fortuna kids and drove them home. Then she hurried out to Wonderland.

* * * * *

Furosa sat in her tent and lit the kerosene lantern. The glow tossed undulating shadows on the dark canvas and made the empty tent look enormous.

110

The wimmin had all gone for a walk in the twilight, and Furooa woloomod tho ohanoo to work on tho "Herstory" series she was going to give at the two-week gathering of womunculture. The wimmin from Side Saddle were expected and countless others from many cities. Furosa popped a lemon sour in her mouth and sucked on it and, placing her note pad close to the lamp, began to make notes.

Irene ducked under the tent flaps — still rolled up in the late-summer heat — and startled Furosa who was deep in thought.

"Irene Aguilar!" she said, patting an empty place on her sleeping platform and offering her a lemon sour.

Irene shook her head and suddenly wondered why she had come. She was embarrassed; she didn't know what to say, where to start.

"I'm glad you could find your way back," Furosa gushed.

"I'm good at directions."

A long and ridiculous silence followed. Irene gazed at the ceiling and watched the shadows dance.

"What brings you out here?" Furosa asked finally, helping herself to another candy.

"I need someone to talk to. I need some advice."

"Dyke talk?" Furosa teased. "I'm listening."

Irene was upset.

"I'm sorry. That wasn't fair. Sure you don't want a lemon drop?

Irene shook her head.

"What's the matter?"

"I'm in love with a married woman," Irene said simply.

Furosa shrugged and continued sucking.

111

Irene cleared her throat. "I'm in love with a married woman," she repeated a little louder and more clearly.

"And she's not in love with you?"

"I don't know. That isn't the point. The point is I'm in love up to here." She gestured with her hand toward her throat, "And she's got two little kids."

"Is this the womun you were telling me about before? The one you met the Fourth of July? Hey, that womun is hurting. It's your duty to set her free. As a decent, upstanding lesbian, it's your duty."

"I'm not . . . what you say. Just because I'm in love with a woman doesn't mean I'm one of those. It's just an accident we both happen to be women. It's not *because* she's a woman."

"Hmph. The hell it isn't." Furosa popped another candy into her mouth and licked her fat sticky fingers. "But I won't argue with you. I will tell you this, Irene."

Furosa's eyes became suddenly somber, her voice chanted softly and steadily while her fat little fingers danced through the flickering light of the lantern. "You need to know your roots. Your roots — our roots — are our herstory, and goddess knows we have a fine one! And through our herstory our culture emerges like a beautiful pentimento, and through our culture comes our pride and through our pride, power and through our power, freedom!"

Irene shivered in the summer heat and swatted a mosquito.

"You'll see, Irene," Furosa continued. Then she smiled and looked jolly and plump again and squeezed Irene. She uncrossed her legs and pulled her hand-woven Mexican skirt down over her fat thighs.

"Joint?" she asked as she reached for some papers and her special stash bag full of memories and marijuana. Irene shook her head. "Oh, I forgot. You don't smoke."

"No." Irene rocked back on the sleeping platform and shoved her hands deep into the pockets of her cut-offs. "I tried it but I just don't like the feeling."

Furosa shrugged and carefully licked her paper.

"I don't know what to do," Irene continued softly. "I'm Catholic and I was brought up to believe that marriage is sacred."

"Irene, life is sacred. I don't care what you want to call it, or what games you have to play with words to make everything okay, but if that woman loves you, and you love that woman, you're a dyke and so is she. And if she's a dyke and trapped in some stinking marriage, she's living a nightmare, you can count on it. Her life is in danger. She's cut off, you know, in that situation, from herself. Cut off from herstory, her culture, her love, her control, and her freedom. She has no future there. Did your Catholic god tell you that marriage is more sacred than life?"

Irene stared thoughtfully at her feet, then turned toward a murmur she could hear in the distance.

Furosa took a toke and held it. Her eyes, red and glass-like, also drifted toward the noise that grew louder. The voices of wimmin talking, whispering, singing. Two voices rose in harmony above the rest.

"Wow!" Furosa whispered.

"That's beautiful," Irene exclaimed. "Who is it?"

"Blackberry and Shrike. Stay and meet them."

"Maybe some other time. I'm too tired tonight. I've got too much on my mind."

Furosa pulled herself up and straightened her

113

skirt. Then she reached for Irene, hugged her tightly and said, "Irene, you know, you're a beautiful womun. I hope you don't end up getting hurt in all this."

CHAPTER XI

"Arliss, this is Irene. Irene Aguilar." Her voice was shaking. "From the picnic."

"Irene," Arliss said, and had to steady herself against the kitchen counter. "I was afraid you might not call."

"I thought we were going to get together. The dinner and movie thing. Do you think you could go this week?"

"What night?"

"How about tomorrow? I can get off at five-thirty tomorrow."

Arliss scrambled through her mind for an excuse to get out of the house without having to drag along either Howard or the boys. Her mother could be sick.

"Arliss? You still there?"

"Sorry. I was just looking at my calendar. Tomorrow's fine." She paused again, trying to think of how to suggest they not be seen in Mobley. "There's El Caballo — a little Mexican place about halfway between here and White Deer. It's supposed to be authentic.

"Sounds good!" Irene laughed. "I'll check the paper for movies in White Deer. There isn't anything that good showing in town anyway."

"Shall we meet there, then?"

"I'll be there."

* * * * *

"I'm going to see my mother tomorrow night, Howard," Arliss said that evening. He looked up at her from over the top of the newspaper.

"Take the boys. I have a PTA meeting."

"I'll get a sitter. Mother isn't feeling well."

"Don't bring anything home."

I won't, she thought, laughing to herself, bring her home.

* * * * *

"It doesn't taste like Mother's home cooking, but it ain't bad," Irene said, wiping her mouth.

Arliss had both elbows on the table and was resting her chin on her folded hands. She smiled at Irene.

116

"I don't know how you can eat those chilis. Don't they burn your mouth?"

Arliss looked beautiful this night, Irene thought. Her auburn hair was pulled back and held at the nape of her neck with a gold clip. The candle on the table threw a shadow in the hollow of her cheeks and her slender fingers looked delicate intertwined beneath her chin. Her voice, soft as velvet, carried the words easily from her mouth. How Irene wished to hold her, her fragile Suzanne! She shivered and then remembered that Arliss had asked her a question. She dropped her gaze to her plate and picked up one of the little chilis and put it in her mouth.

"I hated them when I was little," she said to Arliss. "I don't know when I started liking them. It just crept up on me." She helped herself to the last warm tortilla from the basket in front of her. "I wish these were homemade. You'd love my mother's tortillas. My mother makes the best. In grade school, I used to get little burritos in my lunch — leftover chicken, whatever we had — and the other kids would bargain for them. I made them give me their desserts. I had tortillas all the time at home; they weren't any big deal. But my mother didn't let us have a lot of candy. Some lunches all I had was cake and candy bars. What I wouldn't give for one of those burritos now."

"You had a lot of bargaining power. I'd have given you all my desserts."

"You would have?" Irene looked at her with laughing eyes.

"I'd have given you my whole lunch," Arliss said, chuckling. She twisted her napkin into a little spiral and dipped it into her water glass. The paper slowly

117

absorbed the wetness. Then she looked back at Irene. "Do you speak Spanish?"

"Not much. I understand it. My parents fight in Spanish. My grandfather didn't speak any English — he's dead now — although he understood it pretty well. My grandmother spoke it real well. I wanted to be like my Anglo friends so I refused to answer anyone in Spanish. I did take it in high school, but I got a C. My accent was good but my grammar was terrible. I did better in English!" Irene looked at Arliss and laughed softly. Then she said, still smiling, "Here comes the waitress. You want dessert?"

"There's a Baskin-Robbins in town. You want to get an ice cream?"

"Sure. You know, I'm an ice cream expert. I used to drive an ice cream truck for Spreckles in Los Angeles."

"No kidding! Did you like it?"

"Yeah, I guess I did. Hey! The movie starts at seven-thirty and it's seven now. We better get going. Why don't we leave your car here?"

Arliss thought for a minute. "I better drive it into White Deer. I can park in front of my mother's house."

Irene followed Arliss into town, to an old neighborhood where Arliss's mother lived. The houses all looked alike.

"When my father died," Arliss told Irene just after she slammed the car door and locked it, "the insurance company refused to pay because it was a suicide. That left my mother with only her artistic talent and a social security check that doesn't amount to beans."

"Suicide!"

118

Arliss glanced quickly at Irene. "Yeah. Suicide. My mother says it was the only existential act of my father's life. Ironic, isn't it?"

"I don't guess I know what you mean by that."

"It has to do with acting instead of always reacting. It has to do with creating your own reality and taking responsibility for it."

"Hmmm." Irene nodded.

"In some ways, I'm very much like my father."

"How so?"

"I guess it has to do with courage. Or lack of courage. I don't know."

"I hope you're not totally like him."

"Me too. I know I don't have his musical talent."

"Is your mother home? Could I meet her?"

"She has a literary club meeting on Thursday nights. I'd like you to meet her. I'd like her to meet you. My mother is an outrageous lady. She's very impulsive and very into her art. Once she called me, literally, at three in the morning when she finished a painting she liked."

"It sounds like she has a lot of zest."

"That's a good word for it. Zest. Yes, my mother is full of zest. There's the Baskin-Robbins, by the way."

They trotted across the street to the well-lit store. Its door was open on this warm night.

"Espresso," Arliss ordered.

"I'd like the fresh peach," Irene said. "In a sugar cone."

"Let me taste yours," Irene said.

"I'll trade you bites," Arliss answered.

White Deer had the flavor of a company town, Irene thought. There seemed to be no pride, no

119

personality, no feeling of hope. Mobley, at least, because it was on the river and had a colorful history in prospecting and gold mining, had character you could feel. But White Deer was empty and hopeless and ugly.

"I'm surprised an artist like your mother would live in a place like this," Irene said, licking her ice cream.

"They have good ice cream," Arliss said. "We don't have that in Mobley, unless you count the Dairy Queen."

Irene licked a drip off her hand. "I'm serious. Why would somebody like your mother live here?"

"There's a small counter-culture in the woods around here — communes and such — because the land is cheap and the law doesn't bother you much. Then there's the literary club. Why *it's* here, I don't know. And there's a gallery. I don't know why it's here either. But Mother thrives on all that."

"My mother is so practical. She'd be scared to death if she thought a commune was moving in near her." Irene looked at Arliss and laughed, and melted ice cream ran down her chin. She put a napkin to her mouth, but she felt no embarrassment like she'd felt when she first met Andy. Arliss was easy to be with, easy to talk to. She fit, like that first pair of boots, the way they felt even the first time she put them on. She felt like singing.

The evening passed too quickly. They walked from one end of town to the other, looking in the store windows, stopping in front of the hardware store, wandering through the scrub of the city park. They sat on the swings and talked about how it was when they were growing up in Los Angeles and Coos Bay.

Once or twice, as they strolled about, their arms brushed. Irene felt the thrill of it and noticed that Arliss did nothing to prevent such a thing from happening again.

Irene said in sudden realization, "We missed the movie."

"I don't think we missed anything," Arliss answered. "Irene," she said as she unlocked her car door, "I feel so comfortable around you. I feel like I've known you for a long, long time."

"I've been thinking the same thing," Irene said, holding onto the door of Arliss's station wagon and looking into her face. The urge to kiss her was nearly overpowering. If she moved at all, it would be toward Arliss, and so she froze until she could regain some self-control.

And Arliss, searching Irene's open face, pleaded silently for strength.

* * * * *

"We did absolutely nothing but walk around that boring little town," Irene told Furosa. "But it didn't matter because I was with her."

"You got it bad."

"I know." Irene ran her hands through her hair and grinned stupidly at the ceiling of the tent. "With Andy it was totally different. I was nuts about Andy, but I was kind of in awe of her, too. I mean, Andy is incredible." Irene threw her arms out wide. "Totally incredible. There isn't anything she can't do. Nothing. You name it, she can do it. You break it, she can fix it. She didn't need me."

121

"I know where you're coming from. I've been there myself."

"Andy taught me a lot. I gotta give her that. If it wasn't for her, I wouldn't be here. I wouldn't have my job. It about killed me when that all fell apart."

"I've left and been left enough to know exactly what you mean," Furosa said. "That's partly why I took a personal vow of celibacy. Relationships were too draining and I needed all my energy for Wonderland."

"Arliss is so different," Irene continued. "She's really smart. I love to listen to her talk. Her voice is so soft and the way she looks at me, her eyes smiling all the time, it makes me feel like I'm melting. She went to college, you know. She thinks a lot. But she still looks up to me, I can tell. It's like she's very tender and fragile and she needs me. That feels good."

"Do you think you're just responding to that? Is it an ego thing?"

"Furosa, I love her. I need her because I love her so goddamn much. But you know what's killing me? I don't dare touch her, even a little. It's driving me nuts."

"Why can't you touch her?"

"I'm scared to death I'm making a big mistake. She *is* married. She *does* have two kids."

A chuckle erupting from deep within her bosom, Furosa tore open a bag of M&Ms. "I don't think, from what you've told me, you're making any mistake. Go for it, you fool."

Irene shoved her hands into the pockets of her jeans and looked up at the sky. "I don't know, Furosa. I sure hope you're right."

* * * * *

The coming of fall made heavy demands on Irene's time. Godelski had a third cutting of timothy to get in while the weather still held, and steers to market. He needed seven cords of wood cut and stacked for the big house, and Irene needed at least three for her cabin. Repairs to the barn roof had to be made before the torrential rains started.

Irene had managed to meet Arliss at the Dairy Queen and Arliss had showed up at Irene's cabin one evening with her two boys, but was able to stay for only an hour. And Arliss was now uncomfortable taking Jesse, the older boy, with her when she saw Irene. What she felt for Irene was taking form and had a name and it seemed more and more important that the frequency of their meetings be kept secret.

Irene had even been too busy to see the Fortuna kids. Alta started fifth grade this fall, and only God knew what was happening with Frankie — poor little devil. Just as soon as all the hay was in she'd get a day off and look the kids up.

During the second week in September, the last field was cut. It had been rained on and turned several times before it was baled. Godelski hired Jack Pickle's nephew Tom to help put the hay in the barn, and on this particular day, the second week in September, Tom and Irene shoved the last bale of rain-damaged hay into the metal storage shed. Tom pulled his gloves off and wiped his face before sinking his hayhook into the bale, said goodbye, and walked off to the house to collect his paycheck.

Irene drove the tractor and the hay wagon back to the machine shed where she unhooked the wagon.

She then drove back out to the field to bring the baler in. All the haying equipment was now broken in one way or another, and while she was making a mental list of what each one needed, Godelski came out to get her to do the evening milking.

"Irene, I swear you don't know when to quit. You pick up your check tonight and take tomorrow off."

The day had been long and hard, so when the cows had been turned out and the milking equipment disinfected and put away, Irene called Lou, who had been gnawing on a big leg joint that Marian Godelski had saved for her from a butchering. The dog left her bone reluctantly and kept peering over her shoulder with longing as she slouched toward the car.

"All right, all right," Irene said out loud to the dog. And she tossed the big stinking thing onto the floor in the back seat.

The next day a gloomy drizzle fell. Irene was glad they had gotten all the hay in. If the hay had gotten any wetter, it wouldn't even make feeder hay. She made a small fire in her stove — just enough to warm up the room while she had breakfast — and made a list of the errands she needed to run while she was in town. Get a library card. Buy groceries. Buy oil for the car. Find the Fortunas. She would try calling Arliss as soon as she got there. Perhaps they could meet at the library.

* * * * *

The varnish and wax smell in the library was unusually strong. The librarian, preoccupied, ignored Irene when she walked in. Irene took her coat off in the steamy library heat and nodded and smiled hello

124

to Gracie Blunt, who was poking through some section or other, and wiggled her finger back. Then Irene walked up to the desk to apply for a card. Margaret jumped at the sound of Irene's voice. She was in the middle of planning how Chapters Three and Four would flow into one another, someday.

"Library card," Irene whispered loud enough to be heard.

Margaret smiled at Irene as she handed her an application. There was something refreshing about the young woman's face. Something strong. Something that reminded her of Evelyn. And the more she looked at Irene, the more her heart ached until suddenly she had to sit down.

But Margaret made a point of memorizing the name on the application.

Arliss's car had not been parked in the lot next to the library, so Irene headed for the horse-training books where she could dream. She missed being around horses. People had them around here. Lots of people. But no one she knew.

Gracie had chosen her books and walked by on her way to the check-out desk. Irene knew she was Marion Godelski's sister; she had heard about her long before she ever met her. Herb said Gracie was an odd one, and she was.

Irene knew, without looking, that the person opening the heavy oak library door was Arliss. Their eyes embraced. Their mouths were tight with smiles too big for their faces.

And Margaret saw this — saw them holding each other like this without touching, and she knew. And her heart ached. And at that moment she vowed to find a way to let them know she knew, so at least, in knowing one another, they might corner for themselves some small piece of freedom. And, Margaret added, as a tribute to Evelyn.

"I'm going to check these out," Irene said to Arliss in a whisper. "Then let's go outside where we can talk."

They sat in Irene's car. "So how have you been?" Arliss asked, her head propped up on her hand.

"Busy. This is my first day off in forever. Things should start slowing down now. There's a million things we had to do to get ready for winter. Say, I'm going to try to find Alta. Want to ride along?"

"Sure. I've got a sitter until five. The kids don't get out of school until three. If you have any other errands to do, I'll come with you."

"Do you know if Frankie goes to school? In my school, they had a special class for kids like him."

"There is some kind of program, but I don't think Frankie shows up much, if at all anymore."

Irene got the oil for her car and did her grocery shopping. By the time she was through it was nearly three.

"Who do you suppose takes care of Gussie when Alta's in school?"

"Same person who took care of Alta when she was that age," Arliss said. "Nobody. What is it with you and these kids anyway?"

"I feel sorry for them and I think they're getting a raw deal. They didn't ask to be born."

Alta was crossing the school yard, caught sight of Irene's car and came tearing over to see her.

"Irene, Irene, Irene," she screamed, jumping up and down.

"Hi, kid. How's school going?"

126

Alta stuck her tongue out. "Terrible. Yuck. I hate it."

"Oh, you don't either. Did you get all the stuff you need? Pencils and all that?"

Alta's eyes sparkled. "Just about."

"Did you steal it, you little shit?"

Alta stifled a smile.

"Alta, don't do that. Here, I'll give you the money for the rest of your stuff. What do you need? How much do you need?"

"Hey, Irene, you don't gotta do that," Alta said softly.

"I don't want you stealing. I'd rather give it to you. You can work it off at my house. You can stack my wood or something. Is Frankie here?"

"Heck, no."

"What do you mean, heck no? He should be, dammit."

"Well, he ain't."

"Get in. I'll give you a ride home."

"Hi, Mrs. Ellis. Mr. Ellis gave a big speech today in assembly. You know what he said? I don't remember because me and Lorraine Pickle was passing notes. And plus, there was a whole bunch of fourth-graders sitting in front of us and they never shut up."

"You got a winter jacket?" Irene suddenly asked the kid who was bare-armed on this gloomy fall day.

Alta shrugged.

"Shit!" Irene swore under her breath.

Frankie and Gussie were sitting on the makeshift stairs in front of Sophie's trailer wearing dirty T-shirts and torn jeans.

127

Irene said, "Get your brothers, Alta. You guys gotta have jackets."

"Go to K-Mart," Arliss suggested. "They're having a sale. I got my kids' jackets there."

At K-Mart, Irene paid cash for three jackets and Alta's school supplies. That came to thirty-six dollars. Didn't leave much until next payday. But the kids had to have jackets. Irene let the three of them out in front of their trailer and drove Arliss back to the library for her car.

"Irene," Arliss said as they neared the parking lot. "Are you going to be home tonight?"

"I was planning on it."

"What if I bring over a pizza from Tony's?"

"That'd be fantastic."

"What kind do you like?"

"Any kind. Surprise me. Here's a couple of bucks for my half."

"My treat."

It was dark and the drizzle had turned to rain. Irene stoked up the fire in her cabin and rubbed her hands together. Then she started putting groceries away. Every now and then a raindrop came in around the loose chimney and sizzled on the stove top. A pair of car lights flashed across the window and Irene felt her stomach contract. Arliss would be here in her cabin. They would be alone. Irene stared at the floor.

Arliss knocked quickly and let herself in, balancing a pizza on her left hand. "It's pepperoni," she said and handed the box to Irene.

"I love pepperoni," Irene said as she put the pizza down on the table and opened the box. "You want anything to drink? A beer? Water? Apple juice?"

Arliss sat at the table and rested her chin on her hands. "Just water. I'm trying to lay off the beer."

Irene poured them each a glass of water from a jug that sat on her drainboard, and swung the wooden chair from against the wall around to the table. Alta had said something about Arliss's being drunk a lot, but Irene could not imagine it. She pulled a piece of pizza off for herself and held it up high to break the stringy cheese.

"Tony makes good pizza," Arliss said, her mouth full.

"I'm sorry I don't have anything to entertain you with," Irene said. "I don't have a TV. I don't have a stereo. I could sing for you. That'd be entertaining all right, but you'd probably rather I didn't."

Arliss put down her slice of pizza. Leaning forward, her face serious, she said, "Irene, just being here with you is enough. You have no idea how much your . . . friendship means to me. I haven't felt so . . . *alive* in years."

Irene watched Arliss's face, studied her eyes. As Furosa had said, she had made no mistake. A lump formed in her throat. For the first time since their meeting, she had nothing to say. But she had no doubt that something very dangerous and very beautiful was about to happen.

Arliss reached recklessly across the table and took Irene's hand in hers.

It happened so quickly. One moment they were sitting there, eyes fastened on one another, the next minute they were touching. The room was so quiet that their breath, coming in quick shallow gasps, seemed loud as thunder.

Irene slowly rose and pulled Arliss to her feet. She closed her eyes then and felt her lips touch Arliss's and felt Arliss's hand caress the back of her neck and felt Arliss's body close to hers. Irene disappeared into a world of sensation. Arliss was kissing her now on the face, now on the neck, whispering things into her ear. Irene ran her hands down Arliss's slender arms and caught both her hands. Again they kissed.

Arliss then lifted Irene's hand and placed it beneath her shirt, beneath her bra, against the soft warm flesh of her breast and Irene's knees gave way.

Irene caught herself and withdrew her hand. Then, cradling Arliss's face between her palms, she whispered, "I can't stand up. Let's just get in bed." Her cheeks burned, her ears burned, and there was a burning between her thighs.

Arliss was trembling all over. She clumsily undid the top button of her shirt but couldn't manage the others so she just slipped the shirt over her head. As she stepped out of her jeans she looked up to see Irene's strong, slender body as she stretched to turn the gas lantern off.

As Irene dimmed the light, she looked back at Arliss and smiled. "This thing hisses something awful. I'm going to turn it off. We can see by the light of the stove. There are advantages to having a stove that isn't very tight."

In the glow from the stove, Arliss could see the curve of Irene's face, and she traced the shadow that gave form to the length of her body. In this quiet half-light, they kissed. Arliss shut her eyes to allow her mind the luxury of focusing on nothing more than the utter softness of this woman's lips, of being able to register the very moment that Irene's leg pressed gently between her own, of engaging herself wholly in the sensations that her hands were communicating as they caressed the strong brown body.

Like a symphony, each movement led into the next — adagio, allegro, presto — together, together, together — there, Irene, yes, yes, yes. Where, Irene? Bury my face in your beautiful brown neck. Bury my face in your beautiful, soft breasts. Bury my face on your smooth, strong loin. Bury my face. Bury my face. Bury my face.

"Hold me. Just hold me," she whispered, pulling Irene up to lie next to her. Irene wrapped her arms tightly around Arliss's neck and they laid like that as the muscles of their bodies slowly relaxed.

"Arliss, I love you."

"I love you, too."

Irene kissed her then and pushed the damp hair back from her forehead.

"God! you're beautiful," Arliss said softly, shaking her head slowly. "I hope this is not a dream. But if it is, I hope I never wake up."

"Speaking of waking up, what did you tell your husband?" Irene asked, in a quiet voice. The word sounded strange. Husband.

"I told him I was going to AA."

"For car insurance?"

"That's AAA," Arliss laughed. "AA. Alcoholics Anonymous." She paused for a moment. "I probably should go."

"I can't see that in you. You just don't seem the type."

"Thank you, Irene. I'm glad you, especially, don't think so. But I do have that problem." Arliss propped herself up on her elbow so that she could see Irene's face. "Since I met you I haven't even wanted a drink. I feel high all the time anyway. I keep telling myself it's the first sign I don't really have the disease — that I just have a diseased response to a screwed up situation."

"What are you going to do, Arliss?"

"I don't know, Irene. I don't honestly know."

"How come you got married in the first place?"

"It's a long story. I told you I have no courage."

"What time do you have to be back?"

"I figure those AA meetings probably go until ten or so. You want to get up and eat the rest of our pizza? I can tell you the whole long story while we eat."

Irene got up then and slipped on her jeans and shirt. Arliss dressed while Irene lit the lantern. Irene pulled cold pizza from the greasy box.

Arliss took a deep breath. "In college I was in love with a woman named Martha. We were roommates. We were both freshmen and ignorant as the devil. At first we were just friends, but we were drawn to each other. We got great satisfaction out of sharing our ideas about life. And I respected her deeply. That is a very important thing, respect. We listened to each other. We listened and we heard. We had honest arguments and our search for truth was a genuine one. In those days I believed in truth."

"You don't now?"

"Personal truth, maybe, but probably not ultimate

132

truth. At least I don't believe in it at this time in my life. But I'm very confused right now."

"So what happened to you? What happened to Martha?"

"Because we listened to each other so honestly and so carefully, we actually began to communicate. That sounds silly — of course people communicate. But I mean communicate on a level where the barriers that separate people — the barriers that define loneliness start to disintegrate." Arliss looked hard into Irene's eyes to see if she was making sense.

Irene nodded.

Arliss reached for Irene's hand and squeezed it. How good it felt to talk, really talk, to a woman again.

"One evening we're sitting in our room. We're talking about the idea of self-consciousness, self-awareness — how this idea has struck such terror into human culture, how we've built myths to comfort ourselves. I remember so well . . . We'd lit a candle stuck in an empty chianti bottle.

"We reached for each other at precisely the same moment. A moment of absolute and utter communication. A moment when all we shared mentally and emotionally, we finally consummated physically."

Arliss got up from the table and paced. "As beautiful as it seemed, as perfect as everything felt, as necessary as our relationship was, we knew how the world would judge us. We couldn't reconcile that."

Arliss was quiet for a long moment. She rested her hands on the back of the chair and bowed her head. "We agreed to separate. Martha left before the end of the year. She said she wouldn't be able to stop seeing me as long as there was any way she could. She had to remove herself from me physically. I got a letter from her from Europe and that's the last I heard of her. I don't know where she is now or what she's doing.

"After she left, I fell apart. I started drinking heavily. Then I got disgusted with myself and disappeared into my dorm room for three years. I went from being the class clown to being a four-point student who never smiled. I can honestly say nothing witty ever came to mind. It still doesn't."

Arliss sat down again. "I met Howard in a Russian Literature class. By that time I was so indifferent, nothing mattered. It was time to graduate and time to get married. I didn't give myself a choice."

"Did you ever get used to it?"

Arliss looked at Irene. Her eyes grew hard; they filled with fury. She said through tight lips and gritted teeth, "Irene, I don't suppose, in the beginning, it was Howard's fault. He could not help it he was not a woman. He could not help it that he was not Martha. He could not help it that I did not love him and did not care to be close to him, although, God knows I tried. But then he began to . . . to force himself on me. I started to drink again. Even now, when I have too much, when I can't defend myself, he . . ."

"That bastard!" Irene's fist crashed into the table top.

CHAPTER XII

The fall of '78 fell hard and cold on the Squahamish Valley. The dampness was omnipresent. It saturated the air and the very boards of the houses. It clung to the mountainsides. It crept into the schoolrooms and into the library. Being cold became a fact of life.

Irene rubbed lotion into her raw, cracked hands, wincing as the lotion penetrated an open sore. There was no way to keep her hands dry when twice a day she was washing udders and hosing down the milk room. Then she combed her hair and grabbed her best jacket and, giving her dog a rough pat, headed out into the night to meet Pinky and Esther McGloughlin at Sonny's and pay her rent for November.

The hot tavern air blasted Irene in the face as she opened the door to Sonny's. Smoke poured between the raindrops and disappeared into the darkness. Forest Pickle, drunk already, hung over the bar. Sophie Fortuna was perched on Wild Bill Hunter's lap. Angie from White Deer ordered a drink and sent it over to Wild Bill, but Sophie wrapped her slender fingers around it first and, eyeing Angie over the rim of the glass, raised it to her lips and said, "Thanks."

Angie sauntered over and tapped the glass with her forefinger, splashing whiskey up Sophie's nose. "That wasn't for you, cupcake," she whispered.

Wild Bill roared and dumped Sophie from his lap. Angie grabbed Sophie by the hair. Sophie embedded her fingernails in the side of Angie's face.

"Get the hell out of here," the bartender shouted, pointing to the door.

"I'll take her home," Wild Bill said, laughing, grabbing Sophie by the back of the neck and pushing her roughly toward the door.

Angie dabbed the side of her face with a tissue, then went inside the ladies' room. She shoved her face up close to a place on the mirror where there weren't any cracks. She could see that her makeup was a mess. She dabbed the blood from her cheek with a wet paper towel and put more lipstick on her swollen mouth. Then, tidying her hair, she looked at herself first from one side, then from the other and, apparently satisfied, strutted back into the barroom.

"Wow," Irene said to Pinky and Esther as she

136

pulled a chair up to their table. "I've never seen a bar fight."

Pinky chuckled. "You're not usually in here on Saturday night, neither. Sophie's always good for at least one."

He stubbed out his cigarette and squinted at Irene. "You know them Fortuna bastards pretty good, don't you?"

"They didn't ask to be born," Irene muttered.

Pinky took another cigarette and offered one to Irene. She shook her head.

"That middle Fortuna boy don't know his ass from his elbow," he said, letting the smoke drift up his nose.

"He can't help that," Esther said, tapping the ashes from her own cigarette.

Irene opened her mouth, but then realized that arguing with Pinky would be pointless. She got up to get a beer.

Rain drummed against the window, competing against the jukebox and the shouting and the jostling. Amid the sound of the rain, the screaming of the jukebox, the laughing and shouting of the customers, came a tapping on the window. Something made Irene turn around. She could barely make out in the darkness Alta's face there, her mouth wide open, screaming. Irene jumped up, grabbed her coat, and braced herself for the driving rain.

Alta stood there, barefoot, in a soaked nightgown, crying and shivering. Irene grabbed the child, tucked her as best she could inside her jacket and ran for the car.

Inside the car Irene searched for the blanket. It was on the floor and covered with dog hair. Irene

137

shook it out quickly and wrapped it around the freezing girl.

"Damn Volkswagen heaters!" she cursed, gunning the engine.

"Frankie and Gussie," Alta wept. "Get my brothers."

"Where are they, Alta? What happened?"

"Home under the front steps," she sobbed. "My mom's boyfriend, first he hit Frankie because Frankie didn't get out of the room when he said to. But Frankie don't know nothin', hardly. I always have to help him. Then Gussie peed his bed and cried. I tried to shut him up, my mom got there first and started yelling and yelling. Then this guy hit Gus and I tried to make him quit. He hit me first. Then we all got throwed out." Her teeth were chattering. The streetlights flashed now and again across her rain-soaked, tear-soaked face.

"I'll take you guys to my house. How'd you know where to find me?"

"I didn't. I went out to find anybody and I saw your car."

Irene pulled up to the curb beside the Fortuna trailer. "You stay in here, Alta. I'll get the boys."

Irene slid through the mud of Sophie's yard. A nearby streetlight threw an eerie shadow across the front porch and Irene could see Gussie's leg sticking out from beneath the porch. She called to the boys. Gussie wiggled out backwards and Frankie came crawling out behind him. Gussie wore only his underpants and a pajamas top with no buttons, but Frankie at least had jeans on. Both boys were wet and covered with mud. Irene carried Gus and pulled

Frankie toward the car. She could hear shouting coming from the trailer; all the lights were off but one.

"Get in the back, Alta, and share your blanket with Frankie. Put this around Gus," she said, pulling off her jacket. She glanced at her watch. Midnight. "Damn!" she whispered. If it wasn't so late she could call Arliss and get some clothes for the little one, anyway. She realized she had forgotten to give Pinky the rent money — the very reason she had gone to Sonny's in the first place. He'd be out for it in the morning.

By the time she reached home, the kids had fallen asleep in the back seat. She carefully carried little Gussie, and then Frankie, inside and lay them across her bed, and then led Alta, too big to carry, mumbling and whining, into the cabin. The fire had gone out, so she lit the stove to warm the room, then let her dog in. She spread out her sleeping bag on the floor, patting the foot of it to call her dog, and lay down to go to sleep. Tomorrow was Sunday, she thought just before she dropped off. After morning milking, the day was hers. The kids wouldn't even be up before she got back.

* * * * *

Irene shook the rain from her knit cap as she came back inside the cabin after morning milking. Her watch said six-thirty. It was still dark.

This damn rain, she thought. Shivering, she put some small dry pieces of madrone into the stove. The wood crackled and the stove poured heat from its cast-iron gut. Irene pushed the coffee pot onto the hottest part of the stove top and rubbed her hands together. Gussie whimpered.

"Shh," Irene whispered, and got him up and took him to the outhouse. She waited impatiently until he was through — it was raining hard — then grabbed him and dashed back into the cabin.

"Now go back to sleep," she said, covering him up next to his sister. "It's still early." He looked up at her with confusion and the corners of his mouth pulled down. Irene sat beside him and stroked his matted head and rubbed his filthy little back until he went back to sleep.

Two hours later Irene heard a knock at the door. That's gotta be Pinky, she thought. She opened the door, and the huge man had to stoop to walk in.

The kids were sitting at the table eating bananas and drinking hot chocolate. Pinky removed his rain hat and looked at the kids with surprise.

"Sophie's boyfriend threw them out in the rain last night," Irene explained. "That's why I left the bar so fast. Alta was outside that window yelling for help."

"Y'oughta tell the welfare," Pinky grunted.

"Sophie's not on welfare, I don't think."

"I mean the people that takes care of abuse and such like. Tell the sheriff."

"I guess I will." She reached into the pocket of the wet jeans she had taken off last night and pulled out a wad of bills. "Here's your rent. I meant to give it to you last night."

"S'allright. It's only the second. That's only one day late."

140

"You know I'll pay you, Pinky. You know I always pay you."

"So what're you gonna do with them kids?"

She shrugged. "Take them over to Godelski's for a bath, see if I can get them some clean clothes. Then I guess I'll take them back home. Don't know what else I can do, except for telling the sheriff. I wonder if Sophie even knows they're gone."

"Probably does," Pinky said with a laugh. "She ain't looking no gift horse in the mouth." He put his rain hat back on and opened the door, ducking again to go out.

Irene turned around just as Alta finished sticking her tongue out at Pinky's back.

"What's that for?"

"For him talking about the welfare. He's gross. I hate his guts. Are you really gonna tell the sheriff on our mom?"

"I think I should. I hope you guys don't get sick, spending all that time out in the rain freezing to death."

"Irene, please don't tell." Alta's little black eyes were full of pleading. "They might make us go someplace else. They might make us live in an orphanage. Irene, please, please, please don't tell. *Promise* you won't tell."

"All right. This once. But not if it ever, ever happens again."

Marian Godelski welcomed Irene and the kids with a screen door held wide open, a smile stretched between her ruddy cheeks. Irene carried Gussie into the house.

"Come on, sister, get your brother in here," she called to Alta, who dragged Frankie from the car and up the steps. Marian's two arthritic old poodles walked stiffly from their beds by the stove and gazed opaquely at the children, sniffing their legs cautiously. Her grey cat — the only one she ever let in the house — streaked from its spot under the stove and out the door for the safety of the barn.

"I'll put the dogs in the bedroom," Marian said, picking up both of them in one arm. "They're not used to kids. Go on in the bathroom, Irene. I already got the water running in there." Marian smiled at Gussie as she walked by and tried to get him to smile back, but he clung harder to Irene's neck and hid his face.

"You big baby," Alta said.

Marian waddled back out and shouted down the dark hallway to Irene, "You reckon you can stay for dinner? You could try calling their house."

Irene started to answer but was drowned out when Gus screeched as she tried to wash his hair. She grunted and struggled with him and after she figured he was at least clean, left him in the bathtub playing with some plastic cups.

"Sorry," she said to Marian as she walked out of the bathroom drying herself off. "I had to make him get clean."

"I figured as long as you were here, you might as well stay for dinner."

"I don't see why we can't. After what Sophie did to them last night, she doesn't have room to complain. I don't think she cares anyway." Irene then went back to get Gus so the other kids could get in.

Alta was sitting on the edge of a kitchen chair waiting her turn. She had put Frankie in a chair beside her and he had his head on the table. Marian gently touched his hair.

"You want some hot chocolate, honey?"

"He won't answer," Alta said. "He don't hear you. Not lest you yell right down his eardrum." She was swinging her legs under the chair. "He ain't right."

"Well, do you want some hot chocolate and do you think he would too?"

"If he knew I had it, he'd want it. But Irene already gave us some."

"Well, we don't have toys around. You want to watch TV?"

"Okay."

Irene carried Gussie wrapped in a towel. "I wish I had some clean clothes for this little guy. I hate to put those filthy things back on him."

"Let's give him one of Herbert's shirts," Marian said. "I'll throw their clothes in the washer and dryer. They ought to be dry by the time we get through with dinner. Here, let me take him." Marian had to pry Gussie's little fingers from Irene's neck. "Come on, guy," she said. "I'll get you a big man's shirt." This time he looked at her and laughed.

Irene and Alta tried to bathe Frankie, but he didn't understand what was going on and fought for his life. It took both of them to get his hair clean.

Alta was the last one out. "Irene, do you know how to make braids?"

"Sure."

"Do my hair in braids," Alta said, grinning. Usually her hair just hung in her face.

"I'm no professional, kid," Irene said. "So you'll just have to take what you get. But I'll try."

Alta squirmed in her chair with delight.

The kids sat around the big oak table, the sleeves of their outsized garments rolled up. They didn't look like themselves, Irene thought, with their clean faces and combed hair. Alta and Gus were giggling and acting silly. Frankie stared soberly at his empty plate, waiting for his dinner.

"You guys cool it," Irene said, reaching over to whack Alta on the arm.

"Leave 'em be," Marian said. "They ain't hurting nothing. They're just having fun." She looked at Frankie. "Alta said he don't hear good, bless his heart."

"I figured it was something like that," Irene said. "They ought to be able to help a kid with that, don't you think? You'd think the school would test for something like that."

"Even if they did, Sophie'd have to do something about it and I doubt she would. Ain't it the way it goes, though? Me and Herbert wanted to have kids so bad and never could have any. Except my pets, of course. But other people . . ." She paused, clearly not wanting to talk in front of the kids about their mother. "You know what I mean, they don't want them and can have half a dozen."

144

"No, that doesn't seem fair," Irene said. "Where's Herb?"

"He had to run down to Gracie's. Her plumbing went haywire and there was water, I guess, all over the kitchen floor. Poor Gracie. You know, she don't think clear in an emergency. She gets all flusterated. I had to keep her calm on the phone while Herbert drove down there. I expect he'll be back any time now. He don't like to be late for dinner." Marian gave the kids a couple of cookies each and sent them into the living room to watch TV while they waited for Herb.

The dryer tumbled in the utility room, shaking the kitchen floor. It was easy to tell when the thing shut off.

"It'd be nice if them kids could come here for Thanksgiving," Marian said as she and Irene pulled the clothes from the dryer. "We always have a big old turkey but Gracie's the only family close by anymore."

"It would be nice. But I was thinking about maybe trying to go down and see my folks. I was going to ask Herb if that would be okay with him. I haven't seen my folks for a year."

"Well Lordy me yes you ought to see them. A year is a long time. A year is way too long."

* * * * *

Irene met Arliss in town to help her get things for the boys' Halloween costumes. As Arliss found wash-away hair spray and face makeup, Irene pushed the shopping basket down the aisles at K-Mart.

"Did you ever get these wax lips when you were a kid?" she asked Arliss.

"Who didn't? I don't think they've even changed the flavor. They smell exactly the same."

"I'm gonna get some for Alta and them," Irene said as she picked out three sets of lips, three moustaches, and three pairs of fangs.

Arliss took one pair of lips and pressed them into a pair Irene held. "For you," she said, smiled, and started to put the lips back.

"Wait just a minute," Irene said. "Bring those lips of yours back here." She then pressed her lips against the ones Arliss held. "For you back."

Arliss giggled. "Guess I'll just buy this pair for myself, now that they've been kissed on by the likes of yourself."

"Arliss, I'm so excited to see my folks, but I'm scared, too."

"How come you're scared?" She tossed a bag of chocolate kisses into the basket.

"A lot's happened since I saw them last," Irene said. "For one thing, I know they're going to ask me if I'm dating anyone. They never could understand why I didn't date. Course, I didn't understand either. But I'm afraid something will show in my face."

"I know. I've been through that. Let me pay for this stuff, Irene. Then let's get out of here."

They ordered coffee from Esther McGloughlin at the Frontier Cafe. She looked surprised that they had come in together. "What you doing out tonight?" she asked Irene.

"We were just getting Halloween stuff."

"I don't think you'll get trick-or-treaters way out there."

146

"It's for her and her kids."

"We had a ton last year," Arliss said. As soon as Esther went for the coffee, Arliss whispered, "We can't talk in here. Let's just drink this and leave. We can walk through the fairgrounds."

"I didn't know you two knew each other," Esther said as she put their coffee in front of them and shifted her weight to one hip, getting ready to gossip until another customer came in.

Irene flashed a quick smile at Arliss, covering it up by quickly wiping her mouth with a napkin and clearing her throat. "We met by accident when that fight broke out at the softball game last summer," she told Esther.

"Buddy got hurt in that, you know. First that pitch of Jack's got him a cartesian —"

"Contusion," Arliss said.

"Yeah, one of them. Then he busted his hand in that fight. He couldn't work and he couldn't get workmen's comp, neither. That was something. But I swear, he had it coming. He's always been like that — hot under the collar. Pinky is too, a little. I think the whole family's that way." She shook her head.

Irene had not quite finished her coffee, but got up to leave anyway. It was getting late and she knew Arliss would have to go home soon. She laid a quarter under her saucer and picked up the tab.

"I'll get that, Irene," Arliss whispered.

"I already got it," Irene whispered back.

They left the cafe. Arliss said, "We have to be careful in this town, Irene, not to be seen together too often. Howard is starting to act suspicious. I don't think he believes my AA story anymore. Especially since I'm gone on different nights of the

147

week and more and more often. He's starting to probe."

She ran her fingers through her hair and pushed it back from her forehead. "I'm afraid Howard is going to find out and when he does, the shit is really going to hit the fan. I'm afraid I'll lose the boys."

Irene listened in silence and thought for several minutes. "Arliss, what're you going to do? What's in the future for us?"

"I don't know."

"I think you're going to have to level with him. You're going to have to do it soon if anything is ever going to work out for us."

It was Arliss's turn to walk and think in silence.

"Irene," Arliss said slowly, "I'm not giving up again. If I give up again, I swear it will be over my dead body."

"Let's go back to the car," Irene said, pulling her jacket close to her. "I'm freezing."

CHAPTER XIII

Irene got her hair trimmed downtown at the beauty parlor instead of having Furosa do it, and bought a new flannel shirt to wear home. She got butterflies in her stomach when she thought about seeing everybody. Talking to them on the phone was not the same.

Rita had made cheerleader and was waiting tables at the Ranch Corral after school and on weekends. Rita with a driver's license! It was hard to imagine. Frank had got a promotion at the plant from foreman to yard boss and with it a big raise. Their health was

fine, but Tia Mary — Frank's sister — found out she
had diabetes and was supposed to lose fifty pounds
and then stay on a special diet. If that didn't work
they'd put her on some kind of medicine.

* * * * *

Irene looked at her watch. Twenty-one straight
hours it had been, not counting rest stops for herself
and to let the dog out. Exhaustion had hit about the
time she left San Francisco — she had worked an
extra long day so Herb wouldn't have any more to do
than necessary while she was gone. But she didn't
feel so tired now. It must be a second wind.

Traffic progressively thickened. Where did all the
cars come from? The air was terrible. You couldn't
even see the freeway signs until it was practically too
late. Then the stupid people wouldn't let you over.
Bunch of idiots driving a lot faster and more reckless
than she remembered.

Mission looked the same. And the home street
hadn't changed. By the calendar, she had only been
gone one year. But it felt like half a lifetime.

She signalled left and slowed the car, breathing
deeply. There was the house. They had painted it. It
used to be light blue with dark blue trim, and now it
was tan and brown. The small square lawn was, as
always, freshly mowed. It was greener this year than
last year; the rainfall had finally returned to normal.
Papa had run the edger down the sidewalk. The
family took pride in the way their house looked. Most
people in the neighborhood did.

Irene pulled up to the curb and opened the car

door. The dog knew where she was and ran in excited circles. Irene was so tired and excited she was ready to cry.

She opened the door to the house and set her suitcase down with a thud. Her mother came running out of the kitchen, arms open wide, tears streaming down her face.

"Irene, I'm glad you made it safely. I was so worried. Frank, Irene's here," she yelled toward the back of the house.

Rita came dancing out of her bedroom doing some cheerleading moves. Irene laughed at her. Papa came rushing into the room and hugged Irene, patting her over and over on the back. Rita picked up Lou and carried her around, cooing and bouncing her as lightly as she would a baby.

"I'm exhausted," Irene said as she collapsed into an overstuffed chair. "It was a long drive."

"You didn't drive straight through, did you?" her father asked.

"Well, I did. I can't take too much vacation. The man I work for is left with everything. It's a lot of work. There's a high-school kid he can call in an emergency, but I feel responsible."

"This is a dairy farm you're working on, eh, Irene?" her father said, shaking his head. "I wish you'd find a decent job."

"This is a decent job." Irene heard the challenge creep into her voice. Don't start anything, she said to herself.

"Oh, Irene," her mother broke in. "I wish you'd find a job where you could dress up and look pretty. When you were a baby I used to dress you up so

151

pretty and you liked it so much. The fancier the better."

"You like working at the restaurant?" Irene asked her sister, to change the subject. Rita was still dancing with the dog, waving its paws around in the air.

"It's okay," Rita said. "I don't want to do it for the rest of my life, though. Next year I'm going to the junior college and take bookkeeping."

"Good for you."

"I made you fresh tortillas," her mother said. "I bet you don't get tortillas like this in Oregon."

"Thanks, Mama. I haven't had any good tortillas since I left home. I went out with a friend and ate Mexican food, but it wasn't like yours and they didn't make their own tortillas."

"We were hoping we could talk you into moving back," her father said, leaning his elbows on his knees and folding his hands. "I got a raise — I think we told you that — and I was thinking we could help you go to school."

"Thanks, Papa. I really appreciate that. I might go back to school some day. But I'm not ready yet. I don't know what I'd study. It would just be a waste of your money and my time, I think, until I make up my mind."

"You won't come home, then?"

Irene paused, shifted her gaze around the room, then looked directly at her father in the softest way she could. "I'll come here to visit, Papa. I'll try to come more often, too."

"You're on your own now."

"I'm on my own now."

Her father looked back at her, clasping and unclasping his hands. Irene bit her lip.

They sat down to eat. Fresh tortillas just like her mother had promised. And menudo. You don't get menudo in Oregon, either.

"Irene," her mother said, passing the basket of tortillas for the third time. "You dating anyone special?"

Here it was. Practically the first thing. She bought time by pretending to chew and swallow. She glanced quickly at her mother, then back down at her bowl.

"No," she said, shaking her head at the same time. "I spend most of my time working."

"You need to get a job where you can meet more boys. You aren't going to meet boys in a barnyard."

"If you do, he's bound to be a real pig," Rita said, laughing.

"So who's coming to dinner?" Irene asked.

"Tia Mary and Yolanda. Quatro and Mary Helen. Joe. Frank, didn't Joe say he was coming?" Frank nodded. Rosanne turned back to Irene. "We tried to get a hold of everybody because you're here. Everybody wants to see you."

"What about Linda?"

"Linda will come, too. I told everybody to bring their card tables for the kids. I think all the grownups can sit at the table if we put somebody on every corner, eh, Frank?" Frank nodded. "He just wants to watch football. He bet Joe on the game."

153

That evening Irene lay in her old bed — the very same bed in which she had made the decision to leave home, except now the bed was shoved into a corner to make room for her mother's sewing machine and cutting table. The sheets smelled of the same detergent her mother had always used; it was a brand Irene never bought because it was expensive. Irene stared up at the ceiling, smelling the sheets, thinking about how different her world was from that of her family. She understood theirs far better than they would ever understand hers, even supposing she could ever tell them about it. And that would be true for the rest of her life.

The day after Thanksgiving Irene drove to the mall to go to the record store. It was the same mall she had always gone to, except now it seemed more crowded. More trash littered the parking lot. The record store was still there and even had the same name. But inside, plain as day, was a section for women's music. Had it always been there? How could she have missed it?

"Joan Baez. *From Every Stage*," the kid said as he slipped the album into a sack. "That's an old one."

Irene smiled at him and nodded. When she got outside, she read the back of the album just to be certain she had purchased the right one. There it was, "Suzanne." She'd play it as soon as she got back to her parents' house. Someday, somewhere, she'd play it for Arliss.

* * * * *

Marian Godelski drove to Mobley on Thanksgiving

154

to pick up Gracie because Gracie's old Rambler had quit and no mechanics were on duty because of the holiday. Alta Fortuna passed by wearing a filthy dress and the jacket Irene had bought her. Marian's heart went out to her. Poor child. Wouldn't she just love some of that big old turkey and pumpkin pie?

She waved to the child and Alta's face lit up as she waved both arms. Marian impulsively pulled over.

"Would your mother let you kids come over and eat at our house?" she wheezed.

Alta thought a minute. Then answered carefully, "I don't think so. We're having a big dinner at home."

Alta had lied. Her mother was gone. The boys were gone. Alta didn't even know where they were. But Alta liked the picture of her mother cooking a turkey for everybody like other kid's mothers did for them. It made her feel proud.

Marian was surprised that Sophie would do that. But it was nice. Nice for the kids, for once.

* * * * *

Margaret Mary McGinnis unwrapped one small Cornish game hen and washed it. She had a recipe for wild rice stuffing that would be too expensive if she had to make it for too many people. She and Evelyn used to do this on Thanksgiving. She hummed to herself as she tucked the naked legs inside the tail flap and placed the bird in the oven.

Perhaps in a week or two she would find some excuse to talk to Irene Aguilar who lived at Box 4892 Highway 28 in the old McGloughlin cabin and who had checked out everything by Rita Mae Brown and

Jane Rule and May Sarton that Margaret had ever been able to buy for this tiny under-funded library. She would think of some way to bring that up, and then some way to tell Irene that she needed to talk to women — no, not just women, lesbian women — women like she and Evelyn were. Well, like Evelyn was. Like she is.

If Evelyn were still alive, she would have gone out of her way to introduce herself long before this, Margaret thought admiringly. If it had been Margaret who had died, Evelyn would have grieved loudly on everybody's shoulder and gotten it over with. Then gone on to love again. Margaret could not remember having talked openly since Evelyn's memorial service. She had not cried out loud on anyone's shoulder. It now felt imperative.

CHAPTER XIV

The day Irene left Los Angeles was, in so many
ways, like the day she had left a whole year before. It
was again late fall and the family was gathered on
the sidewalk. But this time, she felt no childish
rebellion. She hugged them all with love, and told
them how good it was to see them and how well they
all looked, and she promised to come back soon. Her
father, she knew, was no longer afraid for her. And
her mother's tears were the ordinary tears of parting
that she would shed each time a daughter left from
now until the day she died, which, God willing, would

be a long time in the future. Irene drove up the street heading north, feeling warm all over.

Four hours later Irene saw the sign for Paso Robles, and an ache appeared out of nowhere and settled inside her. She wondered if Andy still worked at the stable. The wondering grew and became a compelling. Irene turned off 101 and headed out to the Double-L. She checked her watch. Six-thirty. The stable would be closed for sure, even on such a busy day as the Sunday after Thanksgiving. Andy would be tired.

A car Irene did not recognize was parked beside Andy's white pickup. For a moment, Irene's stomach felt tight and she wondered if this was the right thing to do. But the memory of seeing Andy there, just about a year ago, her hair still wet, leaning against a post sipping beer, made her spine tingle. Irene leaped onto the porch. As she approached the door she could hear music playing. She knocked sharply on the heavy door.

"Holy God!" Andy fairly shouted and threw her arms around Irene and danced her around the porch.

Gail came running out to see what the noise was about. She stopped short. Irene hesitated, then threw her arms around Gail and hugged her, too.

"It's good to see you," Gail said, laughing with relief.

"What the hell are you doing in this neck of the woods?" Andy asked excitedly. "Come on in. Gail, we've got beer don't we?" Then, turning to Irene, she asked, "You in a big hurry? Can you stay for dinner? Need a place to stay for the night?" She gestured to Irene's car. "Hey! Don't forget to let your dog out."

158

Then with laughing, teasing eyes, she said, "Will I always have to remind you to let your dog out?"

Irene laughed, too. Things were going to be okay. "I need to get back to work," she said over her shoulder as she opened the car door. "I told my boss I'd be there to milk in the morning — I work on a dairy farm — but I could call him. He'd probably not mind too much as long as I got there before night milking."

"I want to hear what you've been up to," Andy said as Gail came back holding three open bottles of beer. "It's been so long."

"I see you got a couch and a chair that match," Irene said, looking around the room. "And a real bookcase."

"Gail had those."

"Well, what else is new?"

"I got my own beef herd started. Remember that mean old Number Sixteen? I bought her off Wendell. She's a good cow, but Wendell said she was too much trouble for him to mess with. He was just saying that; he was giving me a break. Her calf hasn't turned out bad at all. Remember when we tagged that little heifer?" Andy laughed and laughed. "You should have seen us, Gail."

Irene said, "That was the first shot I ever gave. I've given a hundred since then. Maybe two hundred."

"I'll bet you do on a dairy farm. Anyway, I got me six feeder steers at the auction. Wendell lets me run them with his cattle. I'll do pretty good if beef prices hold up."

"How's my old buddy Cherokee?" Irene asked.

159

"Same. You ought to go out and see him. He's feeling very relaxed right now. He put in one hell of a hard day."

"Hey, when did you cut your hair?"

Andy ruffled her short blonde hair. "When did I cut it, Gail? Was it last month?"

"It was about a month ago," Gail said. "I remember, because you wanted to do something before you went home to see your folks. I think it looks good short, don't you, Irene?"

"Yeah," Irene said, grinning so hard she was almost laughing out loud. "Yeah, I think it looks good short."

"So tell me what you've been up to," Andy said. "Where is this dairy farm?"

"Mobley, Oregon. A few hours south of Portland, right smack on the Squahamish River. And there's this place right nearby called Wonderland. I'm getting my consciousness raised."

"I've heard of Wonderland."

"You have! Where'd you hear about it?"

"From the women's newspaper. What's it called, Gail? *Freewomun Press?*"

"So how are you getting your consciousness raised?"

"The woman that more or less founded Wonderland is a friend of mine. A real good friend."

"Ever get hassled about being Mexican up there? I heard Oregon's redneck."

"For goodness sake, Andy, I'm not Mexican. I was born in L.A."

"You know what I mean."

"Yeah. Just giving you a hard time. No. At least no one's ever said anything to my face. Tell you

160

what, though. They sure don't like the women at Wonderland. When I first got to town I heard wild things about Raging Mother Mountain — that's where Wonderland's at — witchcraft, human sacrifices — people talked like they believed it."

"Raging Mother Mountain. What a perfect place for women's land, don't you think, Andy?" Gail said. "Is that really the name of the mountain?"

"That's the real name. There's some legend about it from the Gold Rush days."

"That's far out Wonderland is so close to where you live. I'd like to see it. Wouldn't you like to see it, too, Gail?"

"You just have to come up and visit me. I'll give you my address." Irene looked around for a pencil and a piece of paper. "Say, I thought of you one day, Andy," she said while she was looking. "I was cutting hay with this super sharp blade. It was laying that timothy down so clean and quiet. And I thought about how pretty you'd think a clean swath like that was."

Andy laughed, and her eyes, her emerald eyes, glistened. "You're sure right about that, Irene."

* * * * *

Irene welcomed her big, damp trees and her muddy driveway. It was so nice not to have to be fighting some jerk in a speeding Porsche for the same small bit of freeway. She was glad to be surrounded, once again, by her big trees and the river and the wild things that crept unseen through the woods. She had missed the hot animal smell of the cows. And the tractor that filled her nostrils, in summertime, with the odor of fresh-cut hay — it was part of her. This was home.

It had been good to see Rita again, Irene reflected. To see all of them. How surprised she had been to realize how pretty Rita was and how nice. You take those things for granted sometimes in your own sister. Rita was a kind person — she cared about people and she was gentle with animals. And Rita was the only person in her whole family who really wanted to hear all about her job and her life in the north woods — she thought it all sounded exciting and romantic. To Rosanne and Frank it was simply a source of worry.

Irene unpacked the dozen fresh tortillas her mother had sent back with her. Tucking them inside a plastic bag, she felt butterflies in her stomach as she thought about sharing them with Arliss. Arliss was going to love them.

But seeing Andy again had been worth the entire trip. It was as though a big piece of her life had suddenly been put back in place. That made her feel strong — strong enough to take on the world — even a world with Howard Ellis in it.

CHAPTER XV

A shaft of sunlight — a rare thing in the
Squahamish Valley in December — caught Margaret
Mary McGinnis's hand as it reached out and came to
rest on Irene's shoulder while Irene was absorbed in
a *National Geographic*. Irene jumped.

"I'm sorry. I didn't mean to startle you,"
Margaret whispered. "I want to ask you a question."

Irene held her breath.

Margaret's voice was low. "Can you and Mrs. Ellis
come to dinner at my house next Sunday?"

Irene closed her magazine and put it back on the

163

shelf. Her throat constricted and her ears burned. She shoved her hands deep into her pockets as she felt her face empty of blood, then fill up again, hot and red. How obvious had they been?

"I'm sorry. I didn't mean to be forward," Margaret stammered.

Irene turned in confusion toward Margaret.

"Please come. We can talk over dinner."

"I'll have to call . . . uh, Mrs. Ellis, and see what her plans are."

"Do you think you could come even if she can't?"

Irene's smile was nervous and she could not keep her lips from quivering. "Sure. I'll come," she answered. And the air was devoid of sound, the library oppressively quiet. Irene shifted her weight, searching for something else to say. "What time?" she finally asked.

"Is five o'clock convenient for you?" Margaret now searched Irene's face with eyes full of apology. She had done a very disruptive thing.

"Five is fine. I'll let you know about Mrs. Ellis."

Margaret agonized over what she had just done. It had not gone at all as she had planned. She had planned to introduce things by discussing some book she knew Irene had checked out — maybe *Desert of the Heart* — and then work around to the invitation. But instead she had just blurted everything out. Anyone would be upset.

Evelyn had had a much better way with people. Margaret was too disturbed over the way she had done this thing to even think about planning any more of her book, and she had been grappling with an important twist in the plot.

164

* * * * *

Rain pounded on the roof. Arliss gathered her rain gear.

"Where are you going?" Howard demanded.

"To see mother," Arliss answered tersely.

"I thought your mother was out of town."

"She was," Arliss said.

"Doesn't Grandma want to see the boys?" Howard asked in an accusing tone.

"She has friends over. The boys would be in the way."

Howard looked at her, and she knew he didn't believe her. And she looked back at him with a hardness that had crept into her and dared him to challenge her. Then she turned away, and without another glance put on her coat and kissed the boys goodbye.

Arliss hid her car on the logging road just off the highway where Irene always picked her up. At the familiar sound of the old Volkswagen putting down the highway, she tightened the ties on her rain hat and ran for the road. Jumping into the car, she looked both ways, then kissed Irene quickly on the lips.

"So what's this all about, love?"

"I don't know. Miss McGinnis just asked us to come to dinner. I was so embarrassed I think I made a fool of myself. Do you think she knows? I think we should be very careful until we know what's going on."

"I'm so happy to be with you, Irene. I don't even care."

165

Irene glanced at Arliss and smiled and squeezed her hand and felt worried because of the way Arliss looked. Dark circles rimmed her eyes. Her skin seemed more transparent and her features, fine by nature, even more delicate.

"Howard is very suspicious," Arliss said. "He wonders why I hardly ever take the boys to see their grandma anymore. I could tell by his face that he didn't believe me." She folded her hands in her lap and stared directly in front of her.

"We need to make plans, Arliss. You can't go on like this and neither can I. It makes me feel seedy, and I don't want to feel that way about us."

"I don't want you to, either. Irene, I wish I knew what to do." She paused, then added, "I guess I do know what to do. I just don't have the guts to just go ahead and do it."

Irene pulled her car into Margaret's driveway. The house reminded her of the one her parents lived in — square, neat, surrounded by a neighborhood full of houses just like it, houses cherished by hard-working folks who took great pride in the few possessions they had managed to acquire. Margaret's driveway was lined with strips of dirt that, in spring, must be wild with flowers.

The porch light was on. Margaret stood beneath it, waiting for them with the door held wide open. She looked stately in a pair of light blue denims and a dark blue button-down shirt.

"Oh, I'm so glad you could both make it," she said, taking first their rain garments and shaking them out on the porch, then their heavy coats.

Three glasses of wine sat on a tray near the

166

entryway. Margaret handed one to Irene and another to Arliss. Arliss hesitated.

"Would you rather have something else?" Margaret asked. "I have juice."

"Thank you," Arliss said.

Margaret then left for a moment and came back with a glass of grape juice. "I should have asked first."

A look passed between Arliss and Margaret, which Irene saw but did not understand. She looked questioningly at Arliss, who smiled back as if to tell her she would explain later.

"Mrs. Ellis," Margaret began.

"Call me Arliss, please."

"Arliss. And I'm Margaret. A Margaret that's always been a Margaret. Not Meg or Maggie or Peg. Margaret. I could never get a nickname to stick, hard as I tried."

"That's like me. But what can you do with Irene?"

"Or Arliss?"

Irene took a drink of her wine and over the top of her glass looked at Arliss. The porch light diffusing through the rain-spattered window illuminated the side of Arliss's face. The cheekbone appeared more exposed and the skin stretched over it, thinner. She looked terribly fragile. Irene's heart ached, and an urge to protect this woman overwhelmed her. She was grateful that she felt strong enough to have something to offer.

Margaret cleared her throat. "I suppose you're both wondering why I asked you over."

She led them into the dining room and reached

for a framed photograph that sat on the table next to a lamp and handed it to them. It was of Margaret when her hair was mostly red, and next to her on a picnic bench was a large and handsome black woman. Their faces were close together and they were holding hands.

"We were together for fifteen years. She died quite suddenly." Margaret's eyes reddened. "Quite unexpectedly about thirteen years ago."

"I'm so sorry," Arliss said softly, and Margaret was touched by the genuine sorrow she heard in Arliss's voice.

"It's been so long you'd think I'd be over it. But I have cut myself off from anyone to talk to. I saw the two of you one day — last September sometime — and the way you looked at each other . . . I'm an old lady, but I know what's going on. I'm not one for doing rash things, but it suddenly seemed vital that I get to know you. There's very little support out there for us lesbians."

Irene shuddered. It would shock Arliss, she was certain, to be talked about that way.

"So many of us don't have our families behind us. We only have each other," Margaret continued. "I finally decided for once in my life I'd take a chance." She took a sip of her wine. "Poor Irene. I really upset you, didn't I? I'm sorry. I had planned to ease into things by maybe discussing something you checked out — *Desert of the Heart*, perhaps. By the way, I have one of the best lesbian libraries in the whole northwest."

Irene couldn't believe an old lady would use that word!

"You're welcome to borrow anything anytime."
She swept her hand down an entire length of her
floor-to-ceiling bookcase.

Arliss scanned the books. She pulled out *The Well
of Loneliness* and flipped through the pages. She
glanced over other volumes — books by Ann Bannon
and Rita Mae Brown, many other writers she had
never heard of. Where had they all been when she
and Martha were so desperately looking for
validation? How could she have missed them?

Arliss slid the book back into its place. "I can just
see me bringing one of these home," she said with a
laugh. "The old book under the mattress trick I used
back in high school."

Margaret nodded. "I had a friend once in a
situation like yours. If she'd been able to get help,
real help . . . but it just wasn't available in those
days. She had a nervous breakdown. The psychiatrists
back then, of course, blamed it all on her being a
lesbian."

Irene winced. She couldn't help it.

"Talk about no support," Margaret added. "Today,
there's little enough. Back then, there was nothing."

"What ever happened to her?" Arliss asked,
reaching for an hors d'oeuvre. She selected an olive
and pulled it off a toothpick with her teeth.

"She got a divorce, but lost custody of their only
child. In fact, the judge restricted Beverly's visitation
rights. She couldn't take the child to her home when
her lover was there. I don't think the law is so
backward these days — you have to remember this
was twenty years ago. She loved that child, too, —
and the whole situation tore her to pieces. But she

eventually got herself together and is, I hope, reasonably happy. But I don't know. Since Evelyn died I've lost touch with her."

"Have you heard of anybody in that situation getting to keep her kids?" Arliss asked, running her finger around the rim of her glass.

Margaret took off her glasses and rubbed her eyes. "I have been so out of touch, I don't know any lesbians anymore, except you two. I would hope things have changed."

The two of us? Irene questioned.

"This is very personal," Arliss said, "and I'll understand if you don't want to answer, but where did you find the courage to . . . uh . . . live your own life?"

Margaret tapped the photograph of herself and Evelyn. "This picture doesn't show the strength of this woman. She was very clear-headed and very stubborn. If it hadn't been for her I probably would be just a lonely old spinster librarian. Of course, I'm lonely once again. But I'm so grateful . . . what did Tennyson say? '. . . Better to have loved and lost than never to have loved at all.' " Margaret's eyes began to fill, so she quickly put the photograph down and walked over to her stereo. She put on Kay Gardner's *Mooncircles*.

"Women's music," Irene said, chewing on a cracker and some cheese. "Everybody in the world must have known about women's music before I did."

"I didn't, Irene," Arliss said. "I still don't. I'm the one who's out of it."

"Gardner is very quiet. It's my kind of music — old lady music," Margaret said with a laugh.

"Have you met any of the women that live out at Raging Mother?" Irene asked Margaret.

"I've seen . . . what does she call herself? Furosa Firechild. The one with the beard. She's been in the library a couple of times. She's the only one I know of. I've always shied away from those types."

"Furosa isn't as strange as she looks," Irene told her. "I know when I first met her I couldn't stop staring at that beard. Now I don't even notice it. Now Furosa is a good friend of mine."

"I didn't mean to criticize. I meant I'm not very adventuresome when it comes to meeting new people." A timer bell dinged from the kitchen. "Dinner's ready," Margaret said and led them to a formal dining table laid with silver and crystal and her best china. "Sit anywhere you like."

As they sat down the rain picked up and hammered away even more vigorously at the windows.

"Margaret, you are an excellent cook," Arliss said, cutting into the perfectly baked salmon.

"Thank you." Margaret bowed her head toward Arliss first, then Irene. "Evelyn would have been out to Raging Mother the day anyone moved in, asking questions, meeting people, making friends. Strange people didn't bother her. She could talk to anybody."

"How did you meet Evelyn?" Irene asked.

"At the University of Idaho. I had just become librarian there. Evelyn was doing research for her doctoral thesis. She was writing it on Northwest Indians and I did a lot of reference work for her. It was very strange, her being there. The northwest — Idaho especially — is a very bigoted place. And even a white woman getting her Ph.D. was a bit of an

171

oddity in those days. After she finished her degree she came back as a research fellow. One of the few women and the only Black the university had ever seen in that capacity, I think."

Arliss took a sip of juice. "Margaret," she began slowly, "with things being as intolerant as they were, how was it . . . living with a black woman?"

"It was wonderful. The living part. With Evelyn. But things were much different back then. Because we were lesbian, we were already living outside the pale, as it were. Our colleagues — people who knew Evelyn — had to like her. She was a charismatic woman. But I don't mean to give you the wrong impression. We were an anomaly and we weren't allowed to forget that. We got phone calls. Notes in the mailbox. But Evelyn was not easily bullied. Evelyn died while Black Power was still in its infancy. I like to believe she would have cut her own path no matter what, but I really don't know. Evelyn was *not* easily bullied.

She paused then and shut her eyes, as if to collect some thoughts. "In my long life I have learned that the external struggles — those struggles against the obvious stupidity of small-minded people — those struggles can take up your time and make your life unpleasant on the outside. They can frustrate you and make you angry. But those struggles cannot compare with ones that rage inside yourself — the ones with self-doubt. It's tough to get a handle on those."

Margaret shook her head and continued. "The outside struggles, they harden you. They force you to define your values and establish your priorities. The ones you have inside just tear you to pieces."

172

Then Margaret laughed softly. "I'm sorry about the long speech. I guess I've had a lot of years to think about things and no one to blab at."

"I had a strange thing happen when I visited a friend on my way back from L.A." Irene said. "This friend asked if I ever get hassled up here for being Mexican. It sounded so weird because I don't feel Mexican inside. I feel American. I was born in L.A., and not even East L.A. I don't know if I'm just blind or what, but I've never noticed anything. Have you ever heard anybody around here say anything about me?"

"No," Margaret said. "But you're not very dark, either. I learned from living with Evelyn that the shade a person is has a lot to do with it. The closer a person looks to a standard white person, the less prejudiced people are. I believe they feel less threatened. It's crazy, but it's a fact. And as long as we're on the subject of prejudice, Irene, your friend Furosa — would you introduce me to her sometime? I believe I've been unfair."

Margaret then got up and went into the kitchen, bringing back little puddings in crystal sherbet glasses. Irene smelled the dessert and took only a tiny bite at first. "This is very good," she said then, cleaning up the dish down to scraping up the last little bits.

Arliss watched her and laughed. "Remember the picnic? I'll never forget your expression when you tried the Brie for the first time."

"Don't make fun of me," Irene said good-naturedly. "You introduced me to something that I like, and it's too expensive to buy very often."

"The store doesn't have it very often, so that takes care of that," Arliss said.

"I'm going to put on some more music," Margaret told them.

It was dark and late before Arliss and Irene got up to leave.

Margaret said, "I want to thank you both for trusting me enough to visit. It has meant a lot to me to have you here. It's been very cathartic."

Irene said, "I'd like to go through your library here sometime. I've read everything downtown."

"I know," Margaret said and they both laughed.

They hugged each other and Irene took Arliss back to her car.

"That was something, huh?" Irene said. "It's funny how you don't think of old ladies being together like that. At least I didn't."

"We'll be old someday, too, and together, if we're lucky," Arliss said.

They were silent for a long time as they drove toward the logging road where Arliss had left her car hidden.

"What was that look you gave me — you know, the grape juice thing?" Irene asked Arliss.

"I hate to tell you. I *especially* hate to tell you." She paused and licked her lips.

Irene put an arm around her. And Arliss told her.

Irene turned onto the logging road where Arliss's car was hidden, and switched off the motor and her lights. In the cramped front seat of the old Volkswagen, they kissed.

"I hate to say goodnight to you," Irene whispered. "Promise me that soon I won't have to."

They held each other and kissed again.

"I've got to go," Arliss said.

And she hated above all else that she had to open the car door. And she hated, beyond that, the thought of reentering her morbid life. If only she were as strong as Evelyn must have been. She kissed Irene quickly once again and ran through the sticky red mud to her car.

* * * * *

"Where were you?"

"For God's sake, I told you where I was going."

"I called there. No one answered. Look at your feet."

"We went to Lily's house. It's out of town. Lily just finished a painting that the Chamber of Commerce in White Deer commissioned."

"Where were you?" His face was hard. Clearly he didn't believe her.

"I told you. Now I'm going to bed."

Howard grabbed her arm. His fingers pressed bruises into her flesh.

"Let go," Arliss said through clenched teeth.

He threw her arm down and went out the front door, slamming it behind him.

It was going to happen soon. How to get ready for it, what to do to plan for something so catastrophic? She didn't know. She felt empty and helpless and desperate.

One of the boys cried from the bedroom upstairs. Arliss lifted her gaze for a moment and let the sound of the crying hurt her. The crying became a whimper and then all was quiet. Arliss poured herself a drink.

At three in the morning, Howard found her there

175

on the living room floor, passed out cold. She groaned once as he carried her to their bed and again when he made her pay for what she was doing to him.

CHAPTER XVI

Irene held Frankie Fortuna's hand until the hearing specialist was ready for him. The special education teacher had said that appointments like this had been made for Frankie ever since he started school, but he had never shown up and there wasn't any more she could do.

"I'll get him there," Irene had promised.

Two weeks later Irene took all the kids with her when Frankie was fitted with glasses that had a hearing aid attached. Frankie's eyes looked huge behind the thick lenses. Alta fussed with moving the glasses up and down on Frankie's nose and giggled, while Gussie stared. The hearing aid had been fitted into Frankie's ear and adjusted, but nothing in Frankie's face showed that it made any difference to him.

"I'll get you guys hamburgers before I take you home," Irene said, and took them to McDonald's. While the kids ate, she found a pay phone to call Arliss and share with her the excitement over Frankie.

"Hello Arliss," she blurted as soon as the receiver was picked up. A man's voice said, "May I tell her who's calling?"

Irene's heart jumped into her throat as she stammered, "I'm sorry," and hung up, her hands shaking. And then she became frightened all over again as she realized how stupid it had been for her to just hang up like that, how much trouble she might cause Arliss just by doing that.

"Time to go," Irene finally said, and she noticed with a rush of excitement that Frankie looked up when she spoke.

The sky was already dark by the time Irene let the kids out, and a few heavy drops of rain mixed with snow splashed against her windshield.

* * * * *

Irene neither saw nor heard from Arliss for nearly two weeks. When she called, either the phone went dead or Howard answered. She knew something was wrong and was terrified that she had somehow made things worse. Then one day at Godelski's, Marian yelled from the house that someone was on the phone for her.

"I have to talk quickly," Arliss said. "Howard's been taking the mouthpiece out of the phone when he leaves and he won't let me answer when he's home. He's accused me of having an affair, but he thinks it's with a man in White Deer. Irene, I need to see you. I miss you so much."

"Can you get away at all?"

"That's why I called. I can get out to go Christmas shopping without Howard or the boys. Meet me at K-Mart tomorrow night at six-thirty."

The parking lot was full. It took Irene ten minutes to find even a small, unmarked spot into which she could squeeze her Volkswagen. She ran through the frozen slush to the big brightly decorated glass doors. Arliss was just inside clutching her coat with her thin little hands, her shivering body defeated by the damp and penetrating cold. Irene's eyes found Arliss's and rested there with joy and relief. It was all she could do to keep from embracing her right there in the slippery entryway.

"Irene, come in here," Arliss said tugging at her arm. "I already know what I'm going to get, so it won't take long. Then let's get out of here."

"Come to my place?"

"Go to your place," Arliss said and laughed.

"God it feels good to be here with you," Arliss said snuggling up in the crook of Irene's arm. "I just can't get close enough."

Irene smiled down at her and tenderly pushed the hair out of her eyes. "We have to start thinking, Arliss. We have to start planning. If we don't, something's going to happen and we won't be ready."

"I try, Irene. I go over and over different scenes in my head. But Howard is always so terrifying in them I can't finish. He will be very vindictive."

"Then we'll have to leave."

"What about my boys?"

"We'll take them."

"Howard will dog me until he finds them. He doesn't want them, but I know he won't let me have them, either. I know that about him."

"Can't you just file for divorce on your own?" Irene asked. "You don't have to mention me. You have reason — you've told me about how he forces himself on you. That's plenty of reason."

Arliss thought for a moment. She had been so limited in her vision by her own guilt that she had altogether overlooked the most obvious solution.

"Irene, you're so practical. But Howard will fight it. He already knows something is going on. He just doesn't know with whom."

"He better never know, either, or we will be up the proverbial creek without the proverbial paddle." Irene sat up and leaned on her elbows. "Changing the subject, is there any chance you could get away

180

again in a couple of weeks? Furosa wants all of us to go to a bar in Portland. The bar's just for women. Furosa says it's a lot of fun. I've never been to a bar like that before. I was going to ask Margaret to come along. She could meet Furosa."

"I'll do it somehow," Arliss said, pulling the covers up around her chin. "God! I've never been to a bar like that, either. Martha and I were too young, not that we would've had the nerve to go to a place like that. We thought we were the only two people like us in the whole wide world."

Arliss pulled Irene down to her and kissed her. "Have your Christmas shopping done yet? Did you get my present yet?"

"Yes, I got your present yet. I got everything done except the Fortuna kids. I mailed my family's stuff yesterday. I kind of wish I could go down and see them, but I can't afford it. Godelski has invited me and the kids to dinner, so I have to ask Alta if they can go. Sophie might actually have something planned. You know, much as I've seen the kids I've never even talked to Sophie."

"You really like those kids, don't you?"

"Yeah, I really do. Hey! I forgot to tell you. Frankie got glasses and a hearing aid. The Lion's Club paid. Isn't that neat? I made Alta promise he gets to school. But the little shit, she doesn't always go herself. But Frankie got signed up for speech therapy. He must be going because he talks a little now. Those kids really should be taken away from Sophie. After that deal in the rain, I should've gone to the sheriff."

"Why didn't you?"

"Alta. She begged me not to. If it ever happens

again, I will. Alta's scared of the welfare. She's scared of being put in a foster home. You can't blame her."

"Irene, you are so beautiful," Arliss whispered and just looked then upon Irene's face. "It's nine. I'd better be going. K-Mart closes at nine and Howard knows it."

* * * * *

Marian Godelski's kitchen smelled of pickles and cinnamon. On the counter two apple pies she had made in the fall and frozen were thawing. Marian stood at the counter arranging two kinds of pickles around radish rosettes. Gracie Blunt was stuffing the turkey. The two old poodles gazed upward, sightless, sniffing the air. Irene was expected soon and was bringing the kids. Marian was excited about having kids around at Christmas time. She had bought each kid a little something, and Irene's presents to them were under the tree, too. Irene had brought something for the old dogs, too, bless her heart.

Irene had told the kids to behave themselves and use their napkins, not their sleeves, to wipe their faces. Just as she pulled up to the back door of Godelski's house, Marian waddled out onto the back porch all smiles and flushed from the kitchen heat, dragging the aroma of the cooking turkey out with her.

"Merry Christmas," she said to Irene. "Ho, ho, ho," she said to little Gussie.

"You're not Santa Claus," he said, pointing to her and laughing. "You don't have a beard."

"But I have presents. Santa left some presents for you under our tree."

Frankie heard her and smiled shyly and put his finger to his lips.

"There ain't no Santa," Alta said and tossed her tangled brown hair.

"If there ain't no Santa, there ain't no present," Marian said to her.

"How come?"

"Don't spoil it for the others," Marian scolded gently, in a whisper. "Let them have their fun even if you don't want to."

Gracie was embarrassed to have so many people around. She was not used to that. But she giggled and fussed and tried her best to entertain, especially the children.

The house felt warm and family-like and Alta pretended this was her family. She pretended that Irene was her older sister and the Godelskis were her parents. Nobody knew she was pretending this.

CHAPTER XVII

Although it was only five-thirty, the sky was utterly black. From the moon, a pale and brittle disc, poured a translucent whiteness that spread like milk over the frozen ground. Irene's breath condensed into a fog around her face.

"Hurry up, Lou," she said, her teeth chattering. The dog was taking her time, the heavy collie-type coat keeping her comfortable in the January chill.

"Get in here!" Irene finally yelled and gave the dog a little shove inside the cabin door with her foot.

Just then she saw the lights of Furosa's van through the trees.

"Lousy heater but good music," Furosa said as Irene shut the door.

"I know. I got a VW, too."

Cris Williamson blasted from seven strategically placed speakers. Furosa was smoking a joint. Irene wondered how that would go over with Margaret.

Furosa tore open a bag of lemon drops with her teeth. Dousing the roach with wet fingertips and placing it carefully in a plastic bag full of other roaches, she dug through her candies and popped one in her mouth.

"Where are we supposed to pick up your friends?" she asked, shoving the lemon drop into her cheek.

"At Margaret's. I'll show you how to get there."

Arliss's car was not parked out in front. Irene's heart beat wildly and her hands began to sweat. What if she hadn't been able to get away? What if Howard had checked ahead of time on her story about having to drive her mother to the airport? What if Arliss had chickened out? Furosa pulled sharply up to the curb, one wheel jumping up on it and sliding back down with a thump. Just then a form came dashing out of the darkness.

Irene leaped from the van and threw her arms around Arliss.

"I had to hide the car," Arliss said, panting heavily.

"I was afraid something had happened."

"It went smoothly. It was spooky it went so smoothly."

Margaret was dressed to the teeth in a bright red polyester pants suit with a grandly ruffled blouse, and

185

she smelled to high heaven of a flowery perfume. She pulled her heavy wool coat from the closet and shut off all the lights in the house but one.

"According to the police," she said, "you should always leave one light on — they say the bathroom, because a burglar never knows when someone might be up using the bathroom in the middle of the night."

Irene introduced Margaret to Furosa. Furosa smiled so warmly and so honestly that Margaret was instantly entranced.

The smell of Margaret's perfume, mixed with the smell of Furosa's musk oil, was heavy inside the closed van. Furosa kept the stereo going until, at nine-thirty, she parked the van in a crowded lot next to the bar. The sign said, WELCOME TO OUR SISTER'S PLACE. Irene shivered, more from excitement than from the cold.

All the way up they had sung with the music and Margaret had sung, too, at the top of her lungs. She felt twenty years younger. She and Evelyn had gone to a bar in Boise on several occasions, and to one in Seattle. She remembered how Evelyn had marched into the bar in Boise so proudly, while she herself had glanced furtively over her shoulder, terrified that someone they knew might see them.

Evelyn had so loved to dance! Margaret felt as though she were paying tribute to her tonight.

Inside the door a woman checked Irene's I.D. and stamped the back of everyone's hands to show they'd paid the two-dollar cover charge. Smoke poured through the open door. The floor vibrated with music. Two huge fans suspended from the ceiling sliced continuously through the yellow haze. Furosa bent her chubby knees to the pounding rhythm and danced herself onto the floor. Margaret's eyes began to water from the smoke. She wiped them at the corners.

Irene stared at face after face in the crowded room. All women! And she was one of them.

A song started — a slow dance — Tina Turner singing "I've been loving you too long, I don't want to stop now . . ." A woman, probably in her early sixties, wearing painter's pants and red suspenders, pushed her way through the crowd and lay a hand on Margaret Mary's arm.

"I only dance the slow dances," she shouted, and took Margaret out onto the dance floor. ". . . I've been loving you a little too long . . . please don't let me stop now . . ." the woman sang softly into Margaret's ear.

To be in the arms of a woman again! Forgive me, Evelyn, for loving you so long! Margaret shut her eyes against the smoke and against the world and melted into a private and beautiful world. For once she did not work on a single chapter of her book.

"Thank you," she said to the woman in suspenders when the song ended. The woman bowed slightly and pushed her way back through the crowd to a table covered with empty beer bottles where her friends were sitting.

Furosa started a circle dance with four other women and soon the dance floor was filled. In the middle of the circle a laughing woman danced with a wooden puppet. Irene elbowed Arliss to look. They were watching, but neither of them could get up enough courage to get out and dance. Furosa danced by and pulled Arliss behind her. Arliss yanked Irene and suddenly they were part of things.

When the circle dance was over, Irene and Arliss stayed out on the floor and giggled as they tried to figure out how to hold each other, joking about who would lead. They danced a silly dance full of dips and twirls, without a thought about who watched and who laughed. They danced a slow dance with their mouths fastened together, their arms holding each other tightly. The music embraced them.

Margaret bought a glass of white wine. The woman in the suspenders motioned for her to come and sit with them. Margaret jostled her way through the crowd and sat down. The woman's name was Bea. It was too noisy to talk, but on the next slow dance, Margaret danced with Bea and felt good again.

At two o'clock the bar closed. "I'm exhausted," Margaret said, rubbing the backs of her calves. "I haven't danced like that for twenty years."

"Who was that woman you were dancing with?" Furosa asked.

"Her name is Bea Denicola. I have her phone number. She lives here in Portland. I'm too old for this!"

"Old, my foot," Furosa said as she pulled the van into the parking lot of an all-night restaurant. "My last lover was sixty-seven. An ex-nun from Grants Pass by the name of Dove. The first time I saw her naked I could not believe my eyes. She was beautiful. Utterly and completely beautiful. Her skin was the color of milk and her tender breasts were small and smooth like two little potatoes. My Dove! My Dove of peace!"

CHAPTER XVIII

"Tell Irene to come in real fast," Marian said to Herb, holding one of her blind old dogs. "Pixie's got a lump. It's right here." Herb felt the mass under the old dog's jaw and shook his head.

Irene came running for the house. Those dogs were so old and decrepit, she had been waiting for something to happen.

"Whyn't you take it down to Dr. Lynn, Irene," Herb said to Irene. "That way if'n a hard decision has to be made, Marian don't have to be there."

"Bring her home, Irene," Marian said. "Even if

it's only so's I can bury her with the rest under that tree yonder. The top of the ground is all that's frozen." Her eyes were wet.

Irene nodded and took the old thing carefully from Marian's arms. Marian went inside to sit in her rocking chair where she could hug the other dog and wait.

The vet felt the tumor and, gazing into the blue-grey opacity of the old dog's eyes, shook her head.

"I didn't think there'd be any use," Irene told the vet. "I don't think they thought it'd be any use, either."

The vet pulled the lower lip of the dog down to expose the rounded canines and the missing incisors. "Do you have any idea how old this dog is? My guess is she's well onto sixteen. The old girl has had a long, and I'm sure, a very happy life. She'll meet her end more peacefully than most of us will."

Irene watched as the assistant held old Pixie while the vet injected an overdose of anaesthetic directly into a vein. Pixie sighed deeply and that was all.

Marian was inside still rocking the other dog when Irene came in. Marian saw the bag and rocked herself for all she was worth and cried her eyes out.

* * * * *

Irene swung by the Fortuna house early on an overcast Sunday morning. Frankie was pushing his Christmas truck around in the mud. The jacket she had bought him in the fall was dirty and already too small.

"Where's Alta?" Irene asked him. He squinted at

her through his thick glasses and pointed toward the house, then he went back to his truck. Irene knocked nervously on the door. She had never met Sophie, and today wasn't the day she wanted to introduce herself. But, as usual, Sophie wasn't home and Alta answered the door.

"Irene!"

"You guys want to come with me to White Deer? I'm getting a puppy for Mrs. Godelski. she had to have her old dog put to sleep last Friday and she misses it a lot. The new puppy's going to be a surprise."

Irene peered inside. It was as bad as she had imagined. One cupboard door hung from a single hinge, the kitchen floor had buckled, and the place smelled of mildew and old food. Gussie was asleep on the couch.

"Leave your mother a note," Irene said.

"She don't care."

"I care. Leave her a note."

Alta grudgingly wrote out a note saying they had gone with Irene and would be back in the afternoon. Sophie wouldn't be home before night, if by then. It was stupid to tell her anything.

The puppy was only half poodle, but it didn't cost anything. Irene handed it to Alta while she drove the twenty miles back to Mobley and on out to Godelski's.

"We have to make this a surprise," Irene told the kids. "You hide out in the car with the puppy, Gus. Alta, you and Frankie come inside with me. I'll tell

191

Mrs. Godelski that Gussie is asleep out here and I'll ask her to come out and get you. Then you hand her the puppy and say 'surprise!' " Alta bounced up and down on the seat and giggled.

A few minutes later, Marian waddled out to get little Gus who was hiding as he'd been told. But the puppy had wriggled free from the four-year-old and tumbled out the door, landing on its chin in the muddy ground. Marian's face froze.

"Surprise," Alta said, holding her hand over her mouth and giggling. "Did you guess?"

Marian couldn't answer. Irene reached down and scooped up the tiny ball of fluff and gently handed her to Marian. Marian pressed it tightly to her, breathing deeply against the tears.

"No papers," Irene said, her own eyes filling.

Marian laughed and cried at the same time. "She'll have papers. Yes, she'll have papers all over the house!"

* * * * *

"Howard, I want a divorce."

Arliss leaned against the back of a living room chair with stiff arms. Howard was reading the newspaper. He slowly lowered it.

"A divorce," he repeated hoarsely. "So you can marry that guy in White Deer?"

"Howard, I want a divorce because I don't want to be married to you anymore," she said evenly. "Our marriage is over. You know that. And I'm not seeing anybody in White Deer except my mother."

"Our marriage never started. You never gave it a chance. Jesus! I should be the one asking for a

192

divorce! And I don't believe you're not seeing anybody in White Deer."

"I'm not, Howard. But I'm not going to prove anything to you. I'm seeing a lawyer."

"Who the hell's going to pay for your lawyer?"

Arliss just stared at him. He had her there. She hadn't thought about how she would pay. She had no job. No money of her own. Her mother didn't have a cent to spare. She didn't even know how much lawyers cost.

"One thing's for damn sure. I'm not footing the bill so you can be free to chip around. That's for damn sure. I'll get a lawyer. And I'll find out who he is, Arliss. No other man's going to raise my boys. I'll guarantee you that." He stood up and walked toward her, shaking the newspaper in her face. Arliss forced herself to stand her ground even though all of her courage had drained out of her. How in hell could she have overlooked a simple thing like paying a lawyer?

* * * * *

Arliss's voice was so weak over the phone that Irene could barely make out what she was saying. The word "hospital" was clear. But who was in the hospital? One of the kids? Her mother?

"I can't hear you. Talk louder." Irene's heart was pounding.

"It's me, Irene. Please come."

Oh, my God! What was the worst thing that could happen? A horrible car accident. Cancer. Irene felt the blood drain from her face and she quickly lowered her head to keep from fainting.

193

"I'm coming now," Irene said, as soon as she could stand up again. She hung up.

Marian was puttering around the kitchen, her new puppy growling and tugging at her pants leg. "You look like you seen a ghost," she said.

"A friend is in the hospital. I don't know. Maybe an accident. I've got to go down there now. Please tell Herb."

"I'll tell him. You hurry."

Irene thought she would never get to the hospital. By the time she parked her car, her hands were shaking so badly she could barely open the door. She felt sick to her stomach. She tore inside and ran to the reception desk, her boots leaving pieces of mud all over the floor.

"I'm looking for an Arliss Ellis," she panted.

"Do you know when she checked in?"

"No, I don't."

"How do you spell the last name?"

Irene leaned over the reception desk to watch the woman's finger run down the list of admissions for the past few days. It stopped, finally. The woman looked over her glasses at Irene.

"Second floor. Room two thirty-five."

Irene opened the door to the private room. Arliss lay in a crib all curled up, facing the wall. Irene stood motionless, a wave of nausea sweeping over her. When she felt she had control she walked in.

"Arliss, I got here as fast as I could."

Arliss turned over and her face said I'm sorry.

"Thank you," she whispered. "Come closer. I need to touch you."

Irene walked over to the crib and reached over the

bars. Arliss stroked her hand and kissed the fingertips. Irene laughed gently, nervously.

"I came straight from the barn, Arliss. You might not want what's on my hands in your mouth."

That made Arliss smile.

"What happened?" Irene asked.

"Irene, please forgive me."

"For what? What's going on?"

"Oh, shit!" Arliss said softly, turning away. She hated herself at that moment more than she hated even Howard.

"Irene, I'm sorry to drag you into this. I think you got more than you bargained for. I'm going to drag you down. I'm sorry . . . I'm so sorry." She was crying.

Irene reached as far through the bars as she could and touched Arliss's hair. She fought for control, and then said, her voice catching, "Arliss, damn it, what the hell have you gone and done? Why didn't you come to me?"

Arliss rolled back toward Irene and laced her fingers around Irene's hand.

"You can at least tell me what happened," Irene whispered.

"Irene . . ." Arliss paused, wondering what words to use. "Irene, I . . . I finally told Howard I want a divorce. He asked me how I was going to pay for it. You know, I never thought about that. The whole ugly thing dawned on me. I was contaminating everyone around me — my babies, Howard, you. I can't live with Howard anymore. I can't drag you into my mess . . ." She lifted her eyes from where they were focused on their intertwined hands up to Irene's face. "The children of suicides are most likely to try it themselves."

"Suicide! Arliss! How? What? What'd you do?"

"I ate all the baby aspirin in the house, that's what."

"How could you do that? How could you do that to me? To us?"

"Oh, please don't be angry, Irene. Not at me. Not now."

"Damn it, Arliss, you should've come to me." Irene dropped Arliss's hand and clenched her fist against her forehead, crying.

"Irene, Irene, Irene," Arliss said softly. "Oh, shit, Irene. I don't want to hurt you. God help me I don't want to hurt you."

"What the hell do you think a stupid trick like that would do, huh?" she sobbed. "Lady, you'd be dead. I'd be the one left hurting, not you. Goddammit, I love you."

Arliss flopped back onto the bed, the back of her hand across her forehead. Irene found a box of tissues and wiped her eyes and blew her nose and tossed the wad angrily into a wastebasket.

"Suicide is very selfish," she told Arliss. "Selfish and stupid." She walked across the room to the barred window and looked out at the misty landscape.

"Irene," Arliss called to her. "Come here, please."

Irene turned and went to her.

"Irene, you're free to go, you know." She searched her lover's face. "Remember about Martha? How we respected each other? How important our mutual respect was? I don't have any respect left for myself and I don't see how you can have any for me, either. Without respect, there can't be love. I won't blame

196

you if you walk out of this room and never come back. But I won't ever forget you, either. And I won't stop loving you."

Irene, her eyes fastened tightly on Arliss's face, felt her anger leave her and her strength return.

"Arliss, I'm not going to leave you. But we've got a big fight in front of us. It ain't gonna be easy, and I can't do it alone." She reached through the bars and stroked Arliss's cheek.

Arliss took her hand and pressed it to her face.

"I promise you, Irene, that I will fight with everything I have."

"How long do you have to be here?"

"Seventy-two hours for observation. Then I get released to my family. I'll go to Mother's. I'm also supposed to go to outpatient therapy. Either find my own shrink or take one they assign to me."

"Shall I tell Margaret and Furosa? Would you like to see them?"

"Yes I would." Arliss looked into Irene's eyes with utter frankness. "But Irene, I don't want to cause any more pain."

"I know, Arliss. I know you don't. But trust me. Please."

* * * * *

Furosa caused a sensation in the reception area because of her beard. Knowing this, Furosa perversely brandished it in the faces of the nurses, stroking it conspicuously when she asked directions to Arliss's room. She popped a cherry sour into her mouth as she waited for the elevator.

Arliss was sitting cross-legged in her crib working

197

a crossword puzzle in the newspaper. The sight of Furosa made her smile. The woman had courage.

"I brought you a book that will make you laugh," Furosa said, and handed her *Rubyfruit Jungle*. "Pass it on to Irene if she hasn't read it already."

"Irene's read this one, but I haven't. Thanks Furosa. I need this. I don't think people actually die of diseases in hospitals, I think they die of boredom."

Furosa dug out her cherry sours and offered one to Arliss. "Have they assigned you a therapist yet?"

"I don't know for sure. Some doctor or other came around today but I haven't actually had a session with anyone yet."

"Be very careful, sister. Male therapists can be incredible pigs. I mean, they're in a position of unbelievable power. They can make you feel like the power to heal lies with *them*." She brought her round, dimpled face close to Arliss's and pointed a chubby finger at her chest. "The power lies within," she said in a forceful whisper.

"Furosa," Arliss said, putting down her newspaper. "How does one find the power? I need it and I can't find it."

"You have just begun to look. There is a woman out there who loves you. There is tremendous power in love. That is the first thing. The second thing is you must get clear on what it is you want." Furosa shut her eyes and placed one finger on each temple. "Keep that vision always in front of you. Always. That way, you cannot get lost."

Arliss reached out and wrapped both her arms around Furosa's neck and held onto her for a long, long time.

"Furosa, thank you. Thank you."

"I have to go. The nurses are waving at me and when they get in that frame of mind, they are dangerous. Take care of yourself, womun. Love *abounds*. Goddess bless."

* * * * *

Margaret was upset, but not surprised when Irene called her at the library to tell her what Arliss had done.

"She wants to see you," Irene said.

"I'll go tonight." Margaret paused a moment, then said, "I was afraid of something like this."

Margaret slowly put down the telephone and rested her chin on her folded hands. At five she locked the library door and drove to the hospital.

"Margaret!" Arliss was dressed and sitting in a chair next to the barred window of her room. It was five-thirty and the horizon was still pink. The daylight lasted longer with each passing week, bringing with it the promise that the winter's rains would soon end. She had been watching the night approach.

Margaret carried a small bouquet of forget-me-nots in a tiny blue vase. "I know you won't be here much longer," she said with conviction.

"I'll take them home with me. Margaret, they're lovely."

Arliss folded her hands in her lap and looked directly into Margaret's lined face. "I really blew it this time."

Margaret looked back at her for the longest time. Nothing she had to say seemed appropriate.

199

Arliss searched her face. "Where did you get your courage?" she whispered.

"From Evelyn." Margaret looked down at her hands that had begun to wring themselves almost of their own accord. "I don't know that I would have had any of my own. I do now, I think. But I didn't back then. It was Evelyn."

"Tell me about her."

Margaret laughed softly. "You'll be sorry you asked."

Arliss patted Margaret on one bony hand. "I want to hear about her."

"I think the most remarkable thing about Evelyn was her ability to love the world in spite of its faults, in spite of all the things she fought to change. Evelyn knew how the world judged her — as a woman, as a black, as a lesbian. But she seemed to separate that from what she saw as her own reality. Somehow — and I never really understood how, although I lived with that remarkable woman for all those years — she loved her womanhood. She was fascinated by her blackness. And the most remarkable thing of all, considering the material most of us have to work with, she was proud and grateful that she had grown up to be a lesbian."

"Proud and grateful. Sounds like Furosa. Furosa visited me yesterday."

"Furosa, too, is a remarkable woman. She and Evelyn would have agreed on many things."

Arliss picked at some lint on her pant leg. "I would like to somehow hook into the hereafter and siphon off some of Evelyn's courage."

Margaret chuckled. "I've wanted to do that many times myself."

Arliss looked again directly into Margaret's face. "You know what scared me? I suddenly realized I hadn't planned anything out. Howard asked me where I was going to get the money to pay a lawyer and I didn't know."

"I understand that kind of fear. That's exactly like something I would do. Always nitpicking about the details that really are of no consequence, and ignoring the real problem. Don't hold it against yourself. Do you have a therapist?"

"Furosa asked me that, too. They just assigned me one this afternoon."

An orderly pushed Arliss's door open with her dinner cart. Margaret stood up to go. "I'll let you eat in peace," she said.

"Thank you very much for coming to see me, Margaret. Thank you for sharing that little bit about Evelyn with me. That helps me . . . a lot." Arliss stood up to give Margaret a hug.

"It helps me, too," Margaret whispered.

"Did you ever call Bea?"

"I haven't yet. But I haven't thrown her number away, either."

* * * * *

Arliss sat in a comfortable chair facing her therapist. He was a small man with narrow eyes and he wore half-glasses. His hands were never still. He tapped his pencil or straightened paper clips or constantly rolled bits of paper into balls.

"What do you think are your strong points?" he asked, turning to a fresh sheet on his tablet.

"My triceps are definitely stronger than my biceps.

201

They never used to be, but they are now." She smiled and folded her hands in her lap.

Irritation flickered across his face. "Strong points of character, Mrs. Ellis."

"I know what you mean. That was just a little joke. I don't have any."

"What would you like to change about yourself?"

"I want more courage."

"Courage to do what?"

"Courage to define my own reality."

"What exactly do you mean by that?"

Arliss stared at this little man.

"What would you say if I told you I'm queer."

"I would ask you why you think that."

"And I would ask you why you don't think that."

He tapped his pencil and stared up at the ceiling, then back at Arliss. "You're getting combative."

"I'm getting the hell out." Arliss rose then and gathered her coat and rain gear. "I hope you have a very nice weekend," she said, and left.

CHAPTER XIX

The songbirds returned to the Squahamish Valley.
The branches were alive with their squabbling and
from the fence posts they sang their hearts out.
Green grass pushed its tender way through the
winter's thatch. Crocuses and tulips bloomed in
Marian Godelski's garden. Marian had chosen one of
the barn kittens to raise in the house with her puppy
so the poor old poodle wouldn't get pestered to death.

Irene was dead tired. At two in the morning Herb
had banged on her door to come help him pull a calf.
All night they had shivered out in the barn, flat on

203

their bellies, their feet hooked around an iron stanchion with the pulling chain between them. The muscles of their arms ached, even though they tried to give each other a rest now and again. And the calf had come out finally, toward four, a bull calf and dead. They thought the cow would be all right. It was amazing how much a cow could take. And they consoled one another that at least it wasn't a heifer calf they'd lost.

"Go on home," Herbert had said to Irene as she poured a little milk for the barn cats. "Marian and I can feed the baby calves."

But Irene said she wouldn't be able to sleep during the day, anyway, so she might as well stay and work. There were a million little things that would need doing before irrigating started. The pump had to be taken into Mobley for an overhaul. The generator on the row tractor needed new brushes. A gate post in the pasture across the river had rotted off at the ground and fallen over.

Irene managed to drop the pump off in Mobley and set a new gate post despite her fatigue, but just as soon as the cows were turned out after evening milking, Irene whistled for her dog and climbed into her car to go home. All she could think of was how good her bed would feel.

* * * * *

Arliss's mother came to the hospital to pick her up, cape flying, silver jewelry flashing.

"I'll quick drive you by your house so you can grab your things," her mother said, giving her a hug.

She smelled, as always, of petoolie. Such a welcome smell!

It was a school day, so Howard was not there. Arliss was grateful for that. The house, she noticed, had not been cleaned nor the dishes done. She packed a few toys along with some necessary clothes. It would take too long to get everything in one trip.

Leaving the house for good — the hated queen bed unmade, the drapes drawn, the lights off, the faint smell of cooked food and dirty dishes lingering in the air — exhilarated Arliss. Even the rain could not dampen her spirits as she and her mother drove to the sitter's to pick up the boys.

The house in White Deer was too small for four people. Money was scarce. Arliss finally found a waitressing job, but after paying her mother for expenses, there wouldn't be much left. Whatever was left would go into her lawyer's fund.

Howard called regularly. Half the time he just wanted to know where Arliss was. The rest of the time he wanted to talk with the boys, although for five weeks, until this weekend, he had not had them even for a visit. He would, he said, fight for custody in court. Arliss, he said, was an unfit mother.

Arliss folded Jerry's sweatshirt and sat on the lid of his suitcase to fasten it. Jerry had insisted on packing his teddy bear but couldn't find it.

"Hurry up, Jerry," Arliss said to him. "Daddy wants to take you to McDonald's."

Arliss was supposed to drop the boys off at

Howard's by six and it was nearly that already. She felt a rush of excitement as she remembered she would then be driving out to Irene's where they would have the whole weekend to themselves. She had not had time to let Irene know, so this would come as a surprise.

Jesse dragged his own suitcase out to the car. "Will you get us on Sunday?" he asked.

"Of course I will," she answered.

He was quiet for the rest of the drive, staring out the car window.

Howard was waiting on the front lawn, impeccably dressed, as usual. He avoided looking directly at Arliss as he took the suitcases from the car and set them inside the house. Then he told the boys to get in his car so they could go out for hamburgers.

"Where are you when I call?" he asked Arliss, still not looking at her.

"I work."

"I've tried all hours of the day and night."

"It's none of your business where I am."

"I think it is. I think it's my business where the mother of my children is. And until those papers are signed, you're still my wife."

Jesse had gotten out of the car and was coming across the lawn toward them.

"Get back in the car, Jess. We're going now," Howard said, and turned, finally, to face Arliss. He started to say something, then with one last angry look, walked away.

* * * * *

The headlights of Arliss's car swept across the

dark trees that lined Irene's driveway. The cabin was dark, but Irene's car was there. Arliss knocked on the door softly, then let herself in. Irene groaned from her bed.

"You all right?"

"I was up all night at Godelski's. Just tired," Irene said, yawning.

"Honey, I'm sorry. You go back to sleep. I'm coming to bed now, too."

Irene's eyes popped open and she sat bolt upright in bed. "You get to stay the night? How did you get away?"

"Howard took the boys. I have the whole weekend."

"That's beautiful," Irene said, her arms outstretched. "I've never seen you in the morning."

"It's not a pretty sight."

"Bullshit," Irene laughed, then, more seriously, asked, "How come Howard took them all of a sudden?"

"I don't know. Maybe he's starting to miss them. Or maybe he thinks it's time he started building his court case. I do think the boys should see him, though. He is their father."

"Come here my love. I'm so tired I can't keep my eyes open any more. And I've got to be up at four to milk. I'm sorry I have to work tomorrow instead of staying here with you. But we'll have Sunday."

"I know. My poor darling."

"Who'd you switch with at work?"

"Nadine. She was tickled to death because you make better tips on the weekend."

Irene sank into a deep sleep with her arms round the woman she loved. Arliss lay awake for a long

207

time just enjoying the smell of Irene's skin, the feel of her body, the warmth of their shared bed. For a brief moment, she thought a light flashed from somewhere outside. She strained her eyes against the darkness, ready to catch it again. Nothing happened. Finally, she drifted off.

"So what did you do all day?" Irene asked, kissing Arliss on the forehead.

"Well, let's see. First I cleaned up the cabin."

"I see that. It looks great."

"Then, about noon, when the rain stopped, I went for a long walk down by the river. It was very peaceful and I did a lot of thinking. I walked down the same path we walked together that day you invited me out for a picnic. It looks different this time of year with the leaves just starting to bud out."

Out of habit, Irene grabbed a bucket to take outside and pump some water to heat for her bath, but Arliss pointed to the stove where a tub was being kept warm.

"Thank you, love," Irene said, and kissed Arliss on the forehead while she shimmied out of her dirty work shirt.

"I made us some stew, too. I don't think the carrots are done."

"We'll eat them raw as soon as I get clean. I'm starving."

"When I was straightening up, Irene, I found this album. Is it the only one you have? I used to have a lot of Joan Baez albums in college."

"If I had electricity, I'd have a stereo, and if I had a stereo, I'd play it for you," Irene said, smiling at Arliss. "There's a song on there I've always wanted to play for you. It's real special to me. It's the reason I bought that album."

"Why don't we take it over to Margaret's? I'll bet she wouldn't mind."

"You watch the stew and I'll run down to Godelski's and call her right now," Irene said, all excited and half scared and embarrassed.

Margaret was delighted to have them come, even though this was the night she had sworn she would actually begin putting the first words of her book down on paper. She hurried to the store to get baking powder so she could make some cookies.

"Joan Baez," she said, looking over the album cover. "Evelyn had her records. Evelyn admired Joan because she never sold out, even after she got famous. I think to this day she is still sticking by her principles."

Irene sat on Margaret's now-familiar tapestry-print couch, her elbows resting on her knees, her palms sweating. Her eyes were fastened on Arliss. Arliss was leaning back in the chair that matched the couch, her head tilted back, her eyes closed.

Margaret carefully dusted the record and set the needle down exactly at the beginning of the song.

> Suzanne takes you down
> to her place near the river,
> you can hear the boats go by
> you can stay the night beside her.
> And you know that she's half crazy
> but that's why you want to be there . . .

"It is beautiful, Irene," Arliss said when the song ended. "Play it one more time and then put on the rest of the album."

Back in the small cabin, Irene lit the gas lantern. "Now tell me why that song is so special to you," Arliss said.

Irene smiled sheepishly. "Arliss, that song gives me chills. I was driving north of Santa Barbara toward Paso Robles — it must have been somewhere around Santa Maria — when this song came on the radio. I swear to God I fell in love with Suzanne. When I first saw you that day, on the Fourth of July, I saw Suzanne. You looked exactly like I had pictured her. Exactly."

"Why don't you just turn that lantern off, Irene. Let's go to bed."

A spring moon shone in the cabin window and lit their faces. Down by the river spring frogs created joyous cacophony. Irene's dog scooted underneath her bed. Irene turned toward Arliss. Her voice was soft in the darkness. "You looked at me, too, on the Fourth of July. I remember."

"Yes I did. I admit it. You looked so strong and so free. Did you know I followed you around all day? There was something about you — I think it was your freedom — that attracted me. I felt so trapped and you looked so free and in control of yourself."

"Arliss," Irene said then in a quiet voice. "I love you. I really, really love you."

Arliss's lips were soft as Irene pressed into her mouth.

210

"Irene," Arliss whispered, "I love you, too."

And the door flew open and crashed against the wall. Lou let out a surprised bark from beneath the bed. Howard stood silhouetted against the moonlit night. The beam of his flashlight caught Arliss in the eyes and blinded her.

"Oh, for Christ's sake!" he said.

Irene's stomach turned to lead. This couldn't be happening.

"Get out," she croaked. Lou shuffled farther under the bed and growled from her dark corner.

Howard shone the beam from Arliss to Irene and back to Arliss. "Get your clothes on," he said. "Get out of here."

Arliss didn't budge.

"For God's sake," he shouted. "You're in bed with a goddamn queer!"

Queer? Irene stared at him. Queer? Who's in bed with a queer?

"Howard," Arliss said, her voice calm and steady, "go home. I know where I am and who I'm with. You go on home."

"Is that it?" Howard said, his voice shaking. "Is that it?"

"Is that why you had me bring the boys over this weekend? So you could follow me?"

He didn't answer.

"You son of a bitch!" Arliss said through clenched teeth.

"I can't believe what I'm seeing," Howard said, again flashing the beam from one face to the other.

"Turn that goddamn thing off," Arliss said. "And get out."

"The boys are staying with me and if you dare

set foot on the place I'm calling the sheriff." Howard slammed the door behind him.

"Oh, shit," Arliss breathed. They sat in the darkness, unmoving, until they heard the car start some distance away.

"Here goes," Irene said, holding Arliss against her.

"The boys, Irene. He's going to keep the boys." Arliss began to sob uncontrollably.

"Just for now, Arliss. Just for now. The divorce isn't even final yet. They're not his yet." But Irene knew deep in her heart that no judge in the country would give Arliss the boys.

CHAPTER XX

"Well, Godelski, I sure as hell wouldn't want no queer diddling my heifers," Forest Pickle said, popping a potato chip into his mouth and laughing. "They'd never take no bull again."

Herb was confused. He'd heard about this unofficial meeting through Pinky McGloughlin. Pinky thought it would be in Herb's best interest to be there. But Herb had not felt so confused and so sad since his mother died. How would he tell Marian? Good Lord, she wouldn't even know what he was talking about!

"She sure took an unusual interest in them Fortuna kids," Herb heard Bill Hunter say. Hunter, of all people. Wasn't he the one that had smacked Gussie around and throwed them all out in the rain?

"Howard Ellis wasn't lying," Bill continued. "I know that. He never comes to Sonny's. Y'all know that. Thinks he's too high and mighty. But he sure was in there last Saturday crying his eyes out and yelling about finding his wife in bed with a queer. Now if that don't beat all!"

"There's more'n one of them in town," Pinky said. "I remember one day Miss McGinnis took the Ellis woman home and that Ellis woman was so drunk she couldn't stand up and that's the truth. Now you tell me what you'd do if'n you had that Ellis woman so drunk. You just tell me what you'd do. And you tell me that old lady didn't do the same goddamn thing."

"There's something funny going on up on Raging Mother," Bill told them. "Ain't no normal woman wears a beard. All of us know that."

"It's the kids I'm worried about," Pinky said. "We got a whole townful of kids. A whole townful. They could have half these kids recruited before you can blink your eye, the way they work."

"Well, we got to clean this town up," Bill said. "We already got trouble. We can't have nothing going on in a library."

"Them Fortuna kids, I know, has been in Irene's cabin over night," Pinky told them. "I seen them there with my own eyes. I told her to call the sheriff and I wondered why she never did. Now I know. She ain't dumb. She ain't gonna turn herself in!"

"Pinky, for crying out loud," Herb protested.

214

"Them kids had been throwed out of their own house. She gave them a place to sleep. She brought them over to my house the next day to clean them up."

"I told you she had them there all night."

"Pinky, you know it ain't anything like the way you're telling it."

"How do I know that?"

Herb sighed and put on his cap. "I ain't gonna stay and listen to this kind of crap."

"We're about to get us a new librarian," Forest shouted after Herbert. "I think you ought to get yourself a new farmhand."

* * * * *

The First Baptist minister preached to a full church about Sodom and Gomorrah, and the Assembly of God was packed with folks who wanted to hear about the wrath of God in the latter days. But down at the Methodist church, one old man talked to a few sleepy folks about love. Love, he said, is what Jesus commanded us to do. Judging, he said, was God's job.

* * * * *

Pinky McGloughlin blocked Margaret's path as she tried to unlock the library door.

"No library today," he said.

"But Mr. McGloughlin, Monday is a library day. Unless, of course, it's a holiday. But today isn't a holiday."

"This Monday is."

Margaret was suddenly terrified. She was old and

215

not strong. She cleared her throat. "Excuse me," she said, but her voice cracked. She tried to shove her key past his arm and into the lock.

"We're getting us a librarian that's normal. You don't work here no more."

Margaret could not believe what she was hearing. She lifted her eyes to meet Pinky's. "I don't know what you're talking about and I don't think you do, either."

Pinky suddenly felt foolish. This old lady, queer or not, was no match for him and he felt stupid to be here, bullying her like this. If he could just get her to go home and stay there. The ones on the mountain, that was a different story. No woman had a *right* to wear a beard.

"Please, Miss McGinnis. Go on home. There's trouble right now. The town's upset right now."

Margaret stared, unbelieving, at Pinky McGloughlin's face.

When Margaret got home she found someone had strewn what was left after a hog butchering all over her front yard.

* * * * *

Irene showed up at four in the morning and began at the far end of the barn, hooking up the milking machines. She noticed that when Herb came in he was acting strangely. His eyes were on her every time she looked at him. And he didn't talk.

At six-thirty Marian always brought them hot chocolate and some little thing to eat — cinnamon rolls, toast, muffins. Six-thirty came and went. Irene felt sick.

216

"Irene," Herb began.

Then he cleared his throat and wiped his mouth. He was clearly uncomfortable. Irene searched his face.

"Irene, there's been some talk in town. Some awful talk. I hate to even tell you what they been saying."

Irene felt terror in the pit of her stomach.

"I ain't even saying I believe them. The story that's been around is that Mr. Ellis went into Sonny's late Saturday night. He don't never go in there. But Saturday he did and he got hisself liquored up pretty good and started talking about why his wife left him. The story he was telling was pretty raw and it had something to do with you."

Herb shut his eyes and clenched his fists. He took a deep breath. "They been saying you two's queer for each other."

"Oh, my God!" Irene breathed.

"I didn't say I believed it. But that ain't the worst part. The worst part is they're saying you been too good to them Fortuna kids."

"I don't believe this is happening." Irene shook her head. "What did the kids say? Didn't they just ask the kids?"

"Sheriff's s'posed to talk to the kids today."

"The kids will set it straight. Alta will tell the sheriff the truth."

"It won't make no difference. They got their heart set on trouble. There ain't no truth nor any more lies for that matter that's gonna change anything now. Irene, I don't believe none of that. You . . . you've been like our family here. And Marian . . . you're it as far as Marian goes. She's in there right now bawling into the hair of that pup you give her."

"Herb," Irene began carefully, looking directly at him, her hand on his shoulder. "What they said about me and Mrs. Ellis . . . Arliss . . . I do . . . I have . . . I am seeing her . . . like that. That's true. I won't lie to you about that. But the kids!" She pounded her fist into her palm. Her eyes filled with tears. How could anybody even think such things!

"Irene," Herb said, taking off his cap and running his hand through his thinning hair. "I don't know about why a girl would fall in love with another girl. It's more'n I can see. But as far as the kids go, I know you ain't done nothing wrong. You done more for them than their own mother or the school or anyone in this town." He lowered his head and rubbed his eyes.

He patted Irene on the shoulder. "I want you to know that me and Mrs. Godelski, we're behind you. You got your job here as long as you want to stay. You can count on that."

The next day Godelski found a first-year heifer with her teats cut off.

* * * * *

Irene was shaking all over as she hung up the last hose from morning milking. What had been done to the cow could not have been done by human beings. The feelings that filled her went beyond anger and beyond sickness and beyond fear. They were new and strange and had no name. What made things worse, Herb had called the sheriff and the deputy they sent to investigate was Bill Hunter's cousin.

Irene knew she could not bring anything more

218

like this on Godelski. She turned to leave the barn, to find him, to tell him goodbye. She nearly knocked him over. He put his arm across her shoulder and that act of tenderness caused her to break down and cry.

"Damn, I'm sorry," she sobbed. He gave her his shoulder.

"It ain't your fault. I talked to Marian. We agree it ain't your fault. Those men are crazy."

Irene stopped crying and wiped the tears from her face with her arm. Godelski handed her a clean handkerchief he pulled from his pocket.

"Thanks." She smiled. "You've been a good boss and I won't forget you. Or Marian."

"Don't get lost, now. You're the best worker I ever had on this place and I hate to lose you. Besides being like a daughter to us. This is killing Marian. You better go say goodbye to her."

Irene blinked back the tears that threatened to start up again.

"You can toss that rag in the washer inside," Herb said and turned quickly away, but not quickly enough to hide his tears from Irene.

Marian's eyes were swollen and her nose was stopped up. "Well, you ain't going to disappear completely, are you? I want you to call and let us know where you are. We'll sneak over and see you."

The half-poodle pup with no papers lay sleeping on a kitchen rug. "That's the cutest pup," Marian said. "The old dog just hates her. But the kitten don't mind." Marian's kitten batted a dust ball around the legs of a chair.

"Marian, I don't know what's going to happen to

the kids," Irene said. "I'm gonna try to say goodbye to them, but if I can't, tell them I tried. Don't let them think I ran out on them."

"We'll keep up with them, Irene. Herb said that night they got throwed out could get them took away from Sophie. Me and Herb, we'd take them kids. They ain't bad kids yet, but if something don't change, they're headed for trouble. Especially Alta."

"Why don't you try. My word won't be good in court, but yours and Herb's will. You might get some of the teachers to testify."

Then, at the thought of what the town was saying, Irene could not help herself and broke down and sobbed. "How can people say what they're saying? How can they even think that?"

Marian wrapped her big red arms around Irene and patted her on the back and helped her cry.

CHAPTER XXI

Filled with anger and confusion and fear, Irene pulled onto the highway and away from Godelski's. Her hands began to shake uncontrollably and then her shoulders. On a logging road just out of sight of Godelski's house, she turned off her engine and leaned her forehead against the steering wheel. She fought the urge to keep rehashing what had happened and forced herself to think about what she must do now, in the next ten minutes.

First, go to the library. Ask Margaret if she could use her home phone to make a long distance call to

White Deer. See if Arliss could help move her stuff out of the cabin. Second, go home and start packing. Third, drive out to Wonderland. If Arliss was able to help her pack, they could plan together what their next move would be.

Irene repeated these few, simple tasks over and over in her mind. Now, she said to herself, start the engine. Drive to the library.

Margaret's old Ford Falcon was not in its customary place and no other cars were parked in the dirt lot. Irene tried the door and found it locked. Her heart sank. Not Margaret, too. Irene raced to her car and sped to Margaret's house.

Margaret was just scraping the last of the mess in her front yard into a big plastic garbage bag when Irene drove up.

Irene ran toward her. "What happened?"

Margaret pushed the entrails into the bag and turned her head away against the stench. Irene grabbed the bag and finished the job, then carried the bag to the garbage can.

"Thank you," Margaret said, wiping her forehead with the back of her hand. "I went to work this morning," she said. Her pale eyes remarkably calm, she related the encounter with Pinky. "It sounds like I'm fired, officially or not, whether it's any of their business or not."

"Margaret, I'm sorry."

"You needn't apologize. They are the ones who should apologize. Sometimes the human race seems so noble, and sometimes it has the brains of a pea. That's not your fault. This may turn out to be a blessing, anyway. It may be just the push I need. I've decided to move to Seattle. There's a book I've been

222

working out in my mind for the longest time. Perhaps this is the time I should write it. I thought I'd call Bea too. Perhaps I'll stay in Portland for a little while."

"I can't believe what's happening," Irene said softly. "It seems impossible that people would do this." She told Margaret about the mutilated heifer.

"That's sick." Margaret shook her head. "That's just plain sick."

"I'll bet it's the same bunch that did this to you."

"I wouldn't be a bit surprised."

"Margaret, I'm scared. I'm scared and I feel like I'm the cause of all of this. It makes me sick to my stomach."

Margaret placed her hand on Irene's shoulder and looked her straight in the eyes. "Irene, the world's sickness is not your fault. I know what Evelyn would say if this happened to her. She'd say, 'This is a wonderful opportunity.' Evelyn could not be defeated, only redirected. I'm going to try that myself, for a change."

Irene smiled. Just talking to Margaret made her feel better. "May I use your phone to call Arliss?"

"Of course."

Arliss answered. "Irene, why aren't you at work?"

"Arliss, something terrible is happening. I have to move out of my place now. After Howard left the other night, he went to Sonny's and got drunk. He was crying and telling everybody in the bar what he'd seen. Arliss, there's a group in town that's trying to run us out. They've done some pretty awful things and I'm afraid of what else they might do. Can you come to my place? I'll tell you about it then."

"I'm supposed to be at work at two, but I'll be there."

"I'm heading home now." Irene hung up and turned to Margaret. "How can we keep in touch?"

"I don't know. Wait . . . I have Furosa's post-office-box number. Let her know where you are. I'll do the same." Margaret reached for Irene and they hugged strongly. "I haven't known you that long, but I feel I've known you well and I thank God for it. In spite of all this . . . this *crap*, Irene, you've been wonderful for me. I thank you for being my friend."

"Take care, Margaret. I'll see you soon."

Irene saw the note nailed to her door as soon as she parked her car. THIS IS A NOTICE TO VACATE, it said. WE WILL BE BURNING THIS FOR PASTURE TONIGHT AS THE BURNING SEASON ENDS SOON.

One day to pack and get out. Irene was relieved. This she had been expecting. After everything else that had happened, it was no surprise.

Irene let Lou out of the car and slapped her side to call the dog to her as she headed for the river. She wanted just to stand there awhile and see if she could recapture one last piece of paradise.

The sky this day was a gorgeous blue. Huge rain clouds congregated in dark groups across it. The rains were coming less and less frequently and soon the summer sun would sear the valley, forcing Godelski and all the other farmers of the valley to irrigate. Irrigating, she thought wistfully. A hell of a lot of work, but it sure is satisfying. Everything stays so green.

The dog walked calmly beside her. Irene tossed a stick into the river, but the dog ignored it. Irene chuckled at her and reached down to pat her on the head.

"You are a worthless mutt," she said. "No kind of watchdog and only half a cow dog. And you can't swim worth shit." The dog wagged her tail slowly and shoved her shoulder into a pile of rotting fish. She squirmed on her back and kicked her legs in the air as she covered herself with the delicious stench. And Irene didn't even try to stop her. She pushed the tender new grass with the toe of her boot. In another six weeks, it would be time for the first cutting of hay. Where would she be then?

She sat down beneath a huge madrone and stared at the river. Thoughts drifted through her mind with little focus. Godelski. The horrible thing they had done to him. Margaret. The horrible thing they had done to her. Things that happened in books and movies, or to other people in other places at other times. Not here, not to her, not to people she knew. The law, she had always believed, would protect the innocent. But the law, she had learned, could be selective about who it chose to protect and under what circumstances.

She didn't feel evil. Stupid maybe. Selfish sometimes. But not evil. She never intentionally hurt anyone.

The sound of a car coming down the driveway brought Irene to her feet. It was probably Arliss, but she couldn't be certain. She walked back toward the house, ready for anything.

She sighed with relief at the sight of Arliss's station wagon. She ran to the car and threw her arms around Arliss's neck. "I'm so glad you're here," she said. "I could've packed by myself, but I need you here right now. I'm scared."

"Tell me what's been going on."

Irene told her about Margaret and Pinky, about herself and Herb and Marian, about the heifer. She showed the horrified Arliss the notice to vacate. "But this is what is really scary," Irene said. "Herb said a bunch of the boys met at the grange hall on Monday to form a group to, in his words, clean up this town. Pinky and a few others have decided my relationship with the Fortuna kids is . . ." She paused while she tried to get her voice together to say the word, ". . . unnatural."

"Irene, that's outrageous!"

"I know that, and you know that, and the Godelskis know that. I think Pinky knows that, too. I even think the rest of the men know that. But Godelski says they've got something in their heads and they're not going to let go of it. It doesn't have anything to do with whether they think it's true or not."

"I'll help you pack. Where are you going? Do you want to come to White Deer?"

"No. I can't meet your mother under these circumstances. I figured right off I'd go to Wonderland. That'll give us time to decide what we're going to do together."

"I understand. Irene, let's get as much of your stuff packed as we can before I have to go to work. I work from two till eight. I'll stay with you out at Wonderland tonight."

226

The sky had filled with dark clouds, and drops began to fall all over the valley. Irene and Arliss dashed between the cars and the cabin with their boxes.

"I think that's most of it, Arliss. You'd better get to work. I'll see you later."

They kissed goodbye.

"Be careful, Irene," Arliss said as she backed up to turn her car around.

"I will," Irene said and waved.

But instead of heading right out to Wonderland, she wandered around her little place until late in the afternoon. The sky cleared finally, but the trees and grass were still damp and the smell of wet pines pungent. With deep sadness Irene finally climbed into her car and drove to Wonderland.

* * * * *

Wimmin had begun to return with the migrating birds. Thundercloud had been in residence for a week and Blackberry for two days. Shrike was there and six or seven others. Word had it Dove was going to spend some time here and Furosa was delighted. Her vow of celibacy might just end!

The road stopped a thousand feet from the tent. Irene pulled in beside the van Furosa drove, amongst the assorted cars of the migrating wimmin. She looked at her watch. Seven-thirty. Arliss would probably be here by nine.

Irene put a leash on Lou before letting her out so

the dog wouldn't go romping through the poison oak. Irene had lots of it on her property, but it wasn't nearly so thick as it was up here. She started up the path to find Furosa.

Furosa was cooking spaghetti over an open fire. "Well, Goddess bless! What brings you out here? Have you eaten?"

"Actually, no," Irene said. She had simply forgotten about it in the rush to get everything packed.

"There's plenty of spaghetti. Help yourself. But there's no ground up dead animals in the sauce." She rummaged through her things until she found a fork and a wooden bowl. Handing them to Irene, she saw Irene's dog standing there looking up at her. "Fed your dog yet?"

"She's eaten. Don't let her fool you."

"Here Lou," Furosa said, handing the dog a piece of bread. The dog took it gingerly, as though from The Dog Poisoner, and a few feet away she spit it onto the dirt floor.

"Ingrate," Furosa said to the dog. Then, turning to Irene, she asked, "So what brings you out here? I know it isn't the Celebration of the New Moon we're having here tonight."

"Furosa, haven't you heard what's going on in town?" Irene asked, her mouth full. The spaghetti tasted good. She hadn't realized how hungry she was.

"I haven't been into town all this week. Tell me."

Irene started from the beginning, and related the entire sequence of events.

"This is very scary," Furosa said and her face was dead serious. "Those pigs are capable of real violence. Do they know you're here?"

"I . . . I don't think so. I don't know how they could. My God! I didn't think about that. Margaret knows. And Arliss knows, because she's supposed to come out here tonight as soon as she gets off work. I expect her in about an hour now. But as far as I know, no one else knows. I'm sorry, Furosa. I didn't think about dragging you into this."

"That's all right, Irene. I didn't mean it that way. I want you here. We can protect you. But we need to know if they're coming."

"They're going to be busy tonight at my old cabin. Pinky and his brother are burning the place down, supposedly to clear a pasture. The boys will all be down there helping them watch the fire."

"Wimmin!" Furosa shouted. "I need everyone here."

The wimmin looked up from their business and slowly gathered in the flickering light of the lanterns near Furosa's cooking fire.

"Wimmin, we could be in danger." The wimmin sucked their breath. "The pig platoon is on a witch hunt. Just down the road, the pigs are burning what used to be our sister's home. Things could get out of hand. We will need scouts and wimmin who will watch in shifts. We need fighters. And we need the blessing of the spirit of the Raging Mother."

"Furosa," Irene whispered, "I really don't think anything's going to happen here. They got rid of me. That's what they want."

"Irene, you didn't think any of this would happen, did you? Did you think they'd do what they did to Godelski's cow? Did you think they'd do what they did to Margaret? Don't take anything for granted. Especially if they start drinking."

229

Furosa raised herself up onto a sleeping platform where she could be seen in the glow of a coal-oil lantern. Head bowed, arms hanging loose from her shoulders, hands fluttering in the fickle glow, she intoned, "In the spirit . . ." Then, raising her fluttering hands slowly and lifting her eyes she continued in the dusky air, ". . . of the Raging Mother . . ." Her arms now were over her head and her hands still fluttered, throwing strobe-like shadows against the tent ceiling, ". . . WE FIGHT . . ." she shouted and the wimmin murmured an echo to her words. Furosa threw her head back and dropped her voice, ". . . for our sister's life . . ." The wimmin hummed. ". . . for the life of the Raging Mother." Furosa dropped her arms and lowered her voice to a whisper. "Oh spirit of the Raging Mother," and the wimmin chanted in unison, "invade our souls." The wimmin's voices lingered in trailing hisses, hanging thinly on the late spring evening.

"Fighters assemble on the south end of the tent, scouts and watchers on the north," Furosa shouted just before she stepped from her platform.

"Wait! Wimmin!" Thundercloud had leaped up. "Three hoots of the Great Horned Owl means you've seen something or done something, but you don't need help. Three hoots followed by the yap of a coyote means help. All right! Let's go!"

Thundercloud led her five scouts into the woods. Blackberry directed the three fighters to fan out from three points near the living area.

From out of the darkness came Arliss just as an orange glow illuminated the night sky. "Help me watch," Irene said, grabbing her hand. "I'll explain."

230

Pinky was going to light the fire. He had two
buckets full of sawdust soaked in diesel to help get
things going. The cabin was old and would burn all
right, but the bushes were still damp from the
sprinkling they had gotten that day. Wild Bill was
watching the east end of the area Pinky said he
wanted to burn. He had a water truck down there.
Buddy was helping Pinky with the side by the road,
which wasn't too hard because the road itself would
be a natural fire break. Jack and Forest Pickle were
on the west. No one was on the river side. There
wasn't any need. No fire that time of year could cross
the river.

Wild Bill also had a case of beer staying cold in
the front seat of the truck. The Pickle boys had
already been by to get themselves a sixpack before
the fire got to where they'd have to start digging and
stamping. With the rain that day, chances were it
wouldn't spread too fast. After four beers, Bill got to
thinking about cleaning up that filthy mountain.
Wouldn't he like to see them weirdos run! Pickle boys
might give him a hand. They knew that land like
their own skin; they'd logged every inch of it.

* * * * *

"I reckon that's Irene's little place a-burnin,"
Godelski sighed. "This is awful. The whole thing is
truly awful."

"Herbert," Marian said, "you remember Pinky
from grade school. You remember how hard he was

on Gracie because of the way she is. He ain't a bad one himself, but he's an easy one to sway."

"I know it. But it just makes me sick. And some of those boys he's got with him are a bunch. I don't know which of them's the one that did that to the cow, but I wouldn't put nothing past that Bill Hunter. And if trouble don't find the Pickles first, they find trouble."

* * * * *

Thundercloud called her scouts to her. "We will meet," she whispered, "every fifteen minutes unless you hear the owl and the coyote. If you're close, move. Otherwise meet. Got it? We'll go in pairs. Each pair's gotta have a watch." Everyone nodded. "You hear hooting and yapping, you move," she repeated emphatically.

Two scouts were sent creeping around the eastern boundary of the land, two around the western one. Thundercloud and the fifth scout weaved their way through the dark trees due north.

Irene, with Arliss by her side, took her place on one of the crucial high points. Lou growled constantly — more, Irene thought, from tension than from anything she heard or saw. Lou had never been much of a watchdog.

Fifteen minutes passed and Thundercloud's scouts reassembled near the tent. "Anyone see anything suspicious?" Thundercloud whispered in the glow of the lantern.

"I saw headlights down on the road," Cedar said quietly. "Of course, that could be anybody."

"You two maybe oughta sneak down the side of

the road a quarter mile each way. Stay up in the trees," Thundercloud whispered to Cedar and White Wing. "If you see a pickup anywhere on the road, unattended, first feel the hood to see if it's still hot. If it is, deflate the tires." Thundercloud looked from Cedar to White Wing to be sure each womun understood. Both nodded to her. "Then let us know. Shrike, you and Star begin a wide circle around the land. Firefly and I will weave our way south."

They disappeared.

The duff was soft underfoot, covered by dead pine needles dampened by the day's rain. Thundercloud could barely hear her own footsteps. Firefly caught her arm. A twig had snapped not a hundred feet from them. Footsteps. Too loud and too careless to be those of a scout.

Thundercloud touched Firefly's arm and motioned for her to stand absolutely still. She could see a man's form moving toward them. Quietly they waited, quietly. From somewhere in the distance, near the road, an owl called three times.

Jack Pickle didn't see a thing until they reached out and tripped him. The only sound he made was a grunt of surprise as he hit the forest floor. A hooting owl held him in a hammer lock while a yapping coyote gathered leaves with gloved hands. From out of the brush sprang a fighter, trained in the martial arts. With her help, the coyote, at great personal risk, stuffed his pants full of poison oak.

"The Raging Mother's Revenge," Thundercloud growled into his ear. "How sweet it is." Then she and the fighter let him up and gave him a push toward the road.

"Dammit!" he swore, as he ran down the steep

233

embankment, frantically ripping at the leaves in his
jeans. "Jesus Christ dammit!"

Forest Pickle did not know where they came from.
Suddenly he was surrounded. He had to laugh out
loud, it seemed so funny. Then he dropped his
diesel-soaked sawdust into the forest duff and turned
to run. And then they got him. Two fighters — one
trained in the martial arts — and two scouts.
    "Don't do that," he screamed. "Oh, shit! Don't do
that!"
    "The Raging Mother sends her very best,"
Thundercloud said with a smile as Firefly put the last
of the poison oak up his shirt, too, just for good
measure.

Furosa crept as softly as her size would let her,
through the crackling brush, through the poison oak.
Her eyes strained against the blackness, looking for
headlights. Her nerves were stretched tight as piano
wires as owls hooted, coyotes yapped in the moonless
distance. She strained her ears, trying to distinguish
the natural sounds from the unnatural.
    She detected a strange odor wafting off the
mountainside. Burning feathers? Old canvas? Rubber?
The tent . . . Goddess bless . . . the tent!
    Furosa whirled and ran as fast as her legs would
carry her back in the direction of her precious tent.
Flames were already licking the poles from where a
lantern had fallen — or been thrown — onto a

234

sleeping platform. A sleeping bag was on fire. Someone was running toward the far end of the tent.

Rage overcame her. Furosa, baring her teeth, screamed like a madwomun, screamed like a mountain lion, screamed like the soul of the Raging Mother exploding from the mountain. She lunged for the running form, paying no heed to the flames that were engulfing Wonderland.

The weight of her brought him to the ground. He could see the flames licking at the tent pole beside him. He could see her bearded face contorted with rage. He realized with horror that, as she pummeled him, she was oblivious to her own safety.

The soles of his boots were melting.

With one tremendous roar, he rolled the fat woman from his body and staggered from the flames.

And the last thing Furosa remembered was the smell of her own burning flesh.

CHAPTER XXII

Pinky's cabin smoldered in the early dawn. An old apple tree that had stood by the back porch but never bore apples was now a black and spiny skeleton reaching morosely for the sky. The fire had never reached the riverbank and Pinky had had to keep dumping diesel fuel on it to burn as far as the road.

Wild Bill, his feet wrapped in wet dressings, his face swollen and covered with scratches, told Pinky something had happened up on Raging Mother Mountain. One of them hippie queers probably knocked a lantern over and damned if it didn't burn the place down. Being as wet as it was, though, the fire didn't go nowhere else.

Pinky told him he better see a doctor about those feet.

"Nah!" he said. "Don't reckon I better do that."

Neither of the Pickle boys was able to work for ten days. Jack finally went in for cortisone shots. The doctor had never seen anything like it.

"How the hell did you ever get poison oak there?" he asked.

Jack's wife had asked the same thing, and he had not been able to come up with a good explanation. And where was the pickup?

It was the source of great puzzlement also to Forest's wife. How could both of them . . .?

The wives went to Sonny's by themselves, being that their men couldn't walk. They spread it around — how their men were laid up — and heard, in return, hundreds of detailed and hilarious ways something like that could possibly have happened.

Those fools would never live this down! Served 'em right, their wives said.

* * * * *

All night long Irene sat with Arliss and Thundercloud in the lobby of the hospital. Furosa had been in the emergency room for hours, it seemed, and

237

they had had no word. No one was willing to leave without word of how she was.

At eight-thirty, the doctor who had been on duty came out to talk to them. He was, by some wonderful stroke of luck, a burn man; he'd treated lots of fire fighters over the years. This was a bad burn, and particularly disfiguring — on the face, and all. He hated to see that on a woman. She'd be in the hospital for several weeks at least, then possibly in and out for skin grafts. They'd have to wait and see. She was sedated and they'd keep her that way for at least the next twenty-four hours. The pain of the burn itself is almost unbearable, the doctor said. The pain of recovery is worse.

Irene promised to bring back information like a social security number and some kind of identification.

* * * * *

Furosa Firechild found herself battling enormous waves of nausea, lost in an ocean of pain in a totally unseaworthy craft. At her feet were gaping holes through which the cold, murky water rushed unstoppably. Her oars were adrift, her compass lost, the danger of drowning imminent.

"Oh! goddess of the mountain," she cried. "Have mercy on me, your landlubbing daughter."

Furosa blinked. Something was rising in the distance, just over the crest of the next wave. Gathering all the strength she had, Furosa raised her head — the water was now up to her neck — and strained her eyes against the sameness of the blue-grey mist and the blue-grey water.

There, treading over the icy brine, her arms extended, her fingers moving in some indistinguishable gesture, was the Raging Mother herself.

As she drew closer, Furosa could see The Mother's lips were moving as though she were saying something, and her fingers, it was now clear, were beckoning to her. Furosa looked around in helpless confusion. Come closer? Are you crazy? Can't you see I can barely move at all? Can't you see how sick I am? My boat is sinking and already the seawater is bubbling from my nostrils.

But the Raging Mother only stretched her lips into a smile and continued to beckon. Furosa, much to her own surprise, was able to sit up. This, at least, got her head and chest out of the water.

The Raging Mother's lips let go of their smile and resumed their word-motions. Furosa listened with all her might, turning first one ear and then the other toward the whispers that still did not rise over the crash of the waves, but were definitely growing louder.

Suddenly, as though someone had turned off the background noise, the voice of the Raging Mother broke through, clear and sweet.

"Watch my hand," she said in a voice as soothing as ointment. The Raging Mother, with the fingernail of the forefinger on her right hand, dug deeply across her left palm, slowly and deliberately at first, then harder and more furiously. The Mother's eyes narrowed as she increased her effort. Furosa watched in horror and thought she would be sick. Suddenly, from the palm of the Mother's weather-cracked hand sprang the most beautiful and perfect jack pine

Furosa had ever seen. It took her breath away.

But before Furosa could adequately admire the Raging Mother's wonderful creation, a cone had grown upon one of the bottom branches of the tree. Another soon followed, and then another, until the entire tree was laden with them.

Once again the Raging Mother took the forefinger of her right hand and dug it deep into her left wrist. But instead of blood spurting from a severed artery, which Furosa had expected, flames shot as high as the Raging Mother's braided head.

Soon the beautiful pine tree was spitting and crackling before her very eyes, the cones exploding like a million firecrackers, casting seeds everywhere.

And then, a most wonderful thing happened before Furosa's astounded eyes. All up and down the Raging Mother's arms, wherever the seeds had landed, saplings grew — millions of them — and each one quickly became even stronger and more beautiful than the mother tree had been.

The Raging Mother then bent over, shoving her face so close to the astonished Furosa that her breath was hot upon Furosa's neck. "The jack pine *must* have fire before it can go to seed," she hissed.

Then, straightening herself, The Mother said in her ointment voice, "Furosa, my Firechild, is my message clear?"

For fully three minutes Furosa stared, open-mouthed, at her tree-covered mother, loving her with all her heart.

"Now," the Raging Mother said in a business-like tone. "Take these and do something useful with them." At that, she ran her dried up old hands all over her body and scraped the trees off like so many

240

toothpicks. Tearing them into lumber, she cast them onto Furosa's lap, saying, "That boat of yours can use some fixing."

* * * * *

"Arliss," Irene said breathlessly, having run from her car into Arliss's mother's house. "I got a job with the Forest Service. I just went down to talk to them and it just so happened some old guy that has worked in range for years just had a heart attack. The job's temporary — but he won't be back this season for sure. They need somebody now, Arliss."

"That's fantastic!" Arliss shouted. "What'll you be doing?"

"You won't believe this — riding horses. I'm not kidding. I'm supposed to make sure the cattle ranchers move their cattle when they're supposed to into the right grazing units. The Forest Service keeps two Appaloosa geldings and a truck and trailer just for that. And I can take Lou. They said I can take Lou as long as no one in the truck with me objects. Four dollars an hour, too. And vacations and sick time."

"That's hardly a job, you lucky stiff!" Arliss said, laughing, catching Irene's neck in the crook of her elbow. "Come here and sit down and help me fill this thing out."

"What is it?" Irene asked, grabbing a kitchen chair for herself, turning it around, straddling it backwards so she could lean her arms against the back of it.

"An application to law school," Arliss said.

Arliss then put down her pen. She leaned her

241

elbow on the table and, running her fingers through her auburn hair, her face serious, said, "I've started seeing a counselor, Irene — a woman in Roseburg."

"I'm glad you finally found someone. Where'd you get her name?" Irene rocked her chair forward.

"From Blackberry. Her name is Freida Chapman. She's a lesbian, which helps. I've only just started seeing her. We talked the first time about me and my boys, and about me and you, and about all our futures. I was forced to face something that's real hard for me. Something I've dreaded."

She paused. Her lips quivered and she blinked hard against the tears. She took a deep breath, wiped her eyes and forced herself to look directly at Irene. "I can't take the boys right now," she said. "I don't have anything to offer them. My own life has to be together before I can help them build theirs. And I don't want them used as weapons. Things are going to be tough enough for them with the divorce and all. Even tougher when they get older and realize their mother is a lesbian."

Irene reached over the back of her chair and took Arliss's hand. "So what *are* you going to do about the boys?"

"I'm going to fight like hell for open visitation. We'll see what happens when they're older and our lives are more together. Maybe things will be different. But I have to be realistic, and I have to do what's best for them."

"You still have to go to court. What are you going to tell the judge about your relationship with me? That's going to come up," Irene said.

"I will tell the judge that you are the best friend I ever had." Arliss paused for a moment, then picked up her pen again and tapped it on her application. "And I'm going to go to law school. Irene, there will be other women who will need the same kind of legal help I need. Well dammit! I'm going to be prepared to help them." She put her pen down and looked up at Irene and chuckled. "Hell, I might even be the judge someday."

* * * * *

The day Furosa was finally allowed to have visitors, Irene and Arliss were there together. Furosa's face was covered with wet dressings. Even her eyes were bandaged. Tubes hung from both arms — one, Furosa explained with difficulty because she could barely move her lips, contained medicine and the other, food. Food served this way, she said, was lousy.

Irene was shocked at how thin Furosa had become. Her elbows were bony masses and her once round fleshy shoulders were now sharp points and deep hollows.

"Zoriah taught me some healing incantations," Furosa said weakly. "I'm supposed to say them at the proper time. But I never know what time it is." Irene heard a small attempt at a giggle. Weak as it was, it was wonderful to hear. It sounded like the old Furosa. But the effort obviously exhausted her.

Furosa touched one tube-laden arm with her hand, then slowly moved the hand up to her face.

"I've lost my beard for good," she said. "That's a hell of a way to shave." She had to rest, then, because talking was so painful. Irene and Arliss waited in this silence while she rested.

"The doctor says burns heal slowly and scar a lot.

But as soon as I can, I'm going to travel all around this country and display this face. I want to show people what we're doing to each other. I want to lecture about this face." Again, Furosa had to rest. Her voice was almost inaudible now. "It hurts," she said, as if in apology. Arliss touched her shoulder.

The nurse was waving them away. Irene took Furosa's hand gently into her own. "They're telling us we have go now. But we'll be back tomorrow." Then she leaned over and placed her lips on the bandage close to where she judged Furosa's ear to be, and whispered, "You are incredible. You make me proud to be a lesbian. You make me proud to be a dyke."

Furosa squeezed her hand then, as tightly as she could, and desperately struggled to keep the pain and the exhaustion from dragging her away so soon.

She drew a deep breath and with all the strength she could muster, whispered hoarsely, "Take care, sisters. Be strong."

When Furosa was finally able to sit up and eat solid food, Thundercloud brought her a box of chocolate-covered cherries.

"Furosa," Thundercloud began. "Where do we go from here?"

Furosa tore open the candy box and stuffed a piece into her hollow face. "Mmmmm, these are good!" she exclaimed, licking her fingertips. Her chin was bright pink where the grafted skin had been attached, and her eyelids drooped — the doctor said from nerve damage.

"Where we go, Thundercloud," Furosa said flatly, "is forward. We dig our trenches deeper. We have no reason to run. We have done nothing wrong. Wonderland is our home. We have a right to be there." She helped herself to another candy. Then, squeezing Thundercloud's face between her bony hands, she smiled and squealed, "Oh, these are yummy!"

"They will fight us," Thundercloud said simply.

"Then we will fight back. We will fight them with weapons they never heard of and have no defense against. We will fight them with courage and tenacity and imagination and humor. And we will educate them."

"You are a dreamer."

"I have always been a dreamer."

Two days before Furosa was to be released from the hospital, Irene and Arliss burst through the door.

"Furosa," Irene said. "Someone's here to see you. Says she met you a couple of years ago."

Furosa looked up to see Karen from Michigan walk through the hospital door. She could not believe her eyes.

"Karen!"

"Aw! Call me Rio de Brazo. While I'm here."

"What the hell are you doing here, womun?"

"I heard the Raging Mother call my name."

"I mean seriously."

"I mean seriously, too," Rio de Brazo said. "Back in Michigan I got into CETA in the carpenter program. There were three other wimmin on the crew with me." She stepped aside and gestured toward the door. "Meet Deb and Rosa and Lotus. I figured y'all probably still needed that shitter, so me and my crew came out here and built you one."

Furosa laughed hard. "Where'd you end up putting it?" she asked, wiping her eyes.

"We built two, actually. One on the path toward the river and one up on the mountainside, with a view," Rio said. "And there's something else, too. With all the wimmin staying out at Wonderland this summer and my crew, we figure we can get a nice longhouse finished by fall. We figure twenty-five by forty. Two-by-six walls. Six inches of insulation. Twelve in the ceiling, of course. And a big hearth for a wood stove. That sound okay?"

Furosa was speechless. She stared at Rio de Brazo and her eyes filled with tears.

The dream, the Amazon dream.

"And as long as we're in the business of surprising the hell out of you," Irene said, "I found out we can get seedlings real cheap from the Forest Service nursery in the spring — enough to replant the whole hillside in pine and Doug Fir."

Then she grinned and, grabbing the sides of her levis, pranced around the room. "The Raging Mother," Irene sang tunelessly, "will dance in her green dress again."

Furosa could no longer contain herself. She wept. Tears of joy. Big, huge, Amazon tears of joy. She threw her head back and, squeezing her damaged eyelids shut, laughed and cried at the same time.

Then she sucked a tremendous lungful of air and let out a yell that was so loud it must have echoed all the way up the hospital hallway and out into Mobley. "Love *abounds!*" the words resounded. "Goddess bless!"

A few of the publications of
THE NAIAD PRESS, INC.
P.O. Box 10543 ● Tallahassee, Florida 32302
Phone (904) 539-5965
Mail orders welcome. Please include 15% postage.

RAGING MOTHER MOUNTAIN by Pat Emmerson. 264 pp.
Furosa Firechild's adventures in Wonderland. ISBN 0-941483-35-5 $8.95

IN EVERY PORT by Karin Kallmaker. 228 pp. Jessica's sexy,
adventuresome travels.   ISBN 0-941483-37-7   8.95

OF LOVE AND GLORY by Evelyn Kennedy. 192 pp. Exciting
WWII romance.   ISBN 0-941483-32-0   8.95

CLICKING STONES by Nancy Tyler Glenn. 288 pp. Love
transcending time.   ISBN 0-941483-31-2   8.95

SURVIVING SISTERS by Gail Pass. 252 pp. Powerful love
story.   ISBN 0-941483-16-9   8.95

SOUTH OF THE LINE by Catherine Ennis. 216 pp. Civil War
adventure.   ISBN 0-941483-29-0   8.95

WOMAN PLUS WOMAN by Dolores Klaich. 300 pp. Supurb
Lesbian overview.   ISBN 0-941483-28-2   9.95

SLOW DANCING AT MISS POLLY'S by Sheila Ortiz Taylor.
96 pp. Lesbian Poetry   ISBN 0-941483-30-4   7.95

DOUBLE DAUGHTER by Vicki P. McConnell. 216 pp. A Nyla
Wade Mystery, third in the series.   ISBN 0-941483-26-6   8.95

HEAVY GILT by Delores Klaich. 192 pp. Lesbian detective/
disappearing homophobes/upper class gay society.
    ISBN 0-941483-25-8   8.95

THE FINER GRAIN by Denise Ohio. 216 pp. Brilliant young
college lesbian novel.   ISBN 0-941483-11-8   8.95

THE AMAZON TRAIL by Lee Lynch. 216 pp. Life, travel & lore
of famous lesbian author.   ISBN 0-941483-27-4   8.95

HIGH CONTRAST by Jessie Lattimore. 264 pp. Women of the
Crystal Palace.   ISBN 0-941483-17-7   8.95

OCTOBER OBSESSION by Meredith More. Josie's rich, secret
Lesbian life.   ISBN 0-941483-18-5   8.95

LESBIAN CROSSROADS by Ruth Baetz. 276 pp. Contemporary
Lesbian lives.   ISBN 0-941483-21-5   9.95

BEFORE STONEWALL: THE MAKING OF A GAY AND
LESBIAN COMMUNITY by Andrea Weiss & Greta Schiller.
96 pp., 25 illus.   ISBN 0-941483-20-7   7.95

WE WALK THE BACK OF THE TIGER by Patricia A. Murphy. 192 pp. Romantic Lesbian novel/beginning women's movement.
ISBN 0-941483-13-4   8.95

SUNDAY'S CHILD by Joyce Bright. 216 pp. Lesbian athletics, at last the novel about sports.   ISBN 0-941483-12-6   8.95

OSTEN'S BAY by Zenobia N. Vole. 204 pp. Sizzling adventure romance set on Bonaire.   ISBN 0-941483-15-0   8.95

LESSONS IN MURDER by Claire McNab. 216 pp. 1st in a stylish mystery series.   ISBN 0-941483-14-2   8.95

YELLOWTHROAT by Penny Hayes. 240 pp. Margarita, bandit, kidnaps Julia.   ISBN 0-941483-10-X   8.95

SAPPHISTRY: THE BOOK OF LESBIAN SEXUALITY by Pat Califia. 3d edition, revised. 208 pp.   ISBN 0-941483-24-X   8.95

CHERISHED LOVE by Evelyn Kennedy. 192 pp. Erotic Lesbian love story.   ISBN 0-941483-08-8   8.95

LAST SEPTEMBER by Helen R. Hull. 208 pp. Six stories & a glorious novella.   ISBN 0-941483-09-6   8.95

THE SECRET IN THE BIRD by Camarin Grae. 312 pp. Striking, psychological suspense novel.   ISBN 0-941483-05-3   8.95

TO THE LIGHTNING by Catherine Ennis. 208 pp. Romantic Lesbian 'Robinson Crusoe' adventure.   ISBN 0-941483-06-1   8.95

THE OTHER SIDE OF VENUS by Shirley Verel. 224 pp. Luminous, romantic love story.   ISBN 0-941483-07-X   8.95

DREAMS AND SWORDS by Katherine V. Forrest. 192 pp. Romantic, erotic, imaginative stories.   ISBN 0-941483-03-7   8.95

MEMORY BOARD by Jane Rule. 336 pp. Memorable novel about an aging Lesbian couple.   ISBN 0-941483-02-9   8.95

THE ALWAYS ANONYMOUS BEAST by Lauren Wright Douglas. 224 pp. A Caitlin Reese mystery. First in a series.
ISBN 0-941483-04-5   8.95

SEARCHING FOR SPRING by Patricia A. Murphy. 224 pp. Novel about the recovery of love.   ISBN 0-941483-00-2   8.95

DUSTY'S QUEEN OF HEARTS DINER by Lee Lynch. 240 pp. Romantic blue-collar novel.   ISBN 0-941483-01-0   8.95

PARENTS MATTER by Ann Muller. 240 pp. Parents' relationships with Lesbian daughters and gay sons.
ISBN 0-930044-91-6   9.95

THE PEARLS by Shelley Smith. 176 pp. Passion and fun in the Caribbean sun.   ISBN 0-930044-93-2   7.95

MAGDALENA by Sarah Aldridge. 352 pp. Epic Lesbian novel set on three continents.   ISBN 0-930044-99-1   8.95

THE BLACK AND WHITE OF IT by Ann Allen Shockley.
144 pp. Short stories. ISBN 0-930044-96-7   7.95

SAY JESUS AND COME TO ME by Ann Allen Shockley. 288
pp. Contemporary romance. ISBN 0-930044-98-3   8.95

LOVING HER by Ann Allen Shockley. 192 pp. Romantic love
story. ISBN 0-930044-97-5   7.95

MURDER AT THE NIGHTWOOD BAR by Katherine V.
Forrest. 240 pp. A Kate Delafield mystery. Second in a series.
ISBN 0-930044-92-4   8.95

ZOE'S BOOK by Gail Pass. 224 pp. Passionate, obsessive love
story. ISBN 0-930044-95-9   7.95

WINGED DANCER by Camarin Grae. 228 pp. Erotic Lesbian
adventure story. ISBN 0-930044-88-6   8.95

PAZ by Camarin Grae. 336 pp. Romantic Lesbian adventurer
with the power to change the world. ISBN 0-930044-89-4   8.95

SOUL SNATCHER by Camarin Grae. 224 pp. A puzzle, an
adventure, a mystery — Lesbian romance. ISBN 0-930044-90-8   8.95

THE LOVE OF GOOD WOMEN by Isabel Miller. 224 pp.
Long-awaited new novel by the author of the beloved *Patience
and Sarah*. ISBN 0-930044-81-9   8.95

THE HOUSE AT PELHAM FALLS by Brenda Weathers. 240
pp. Suspenseful Lesbian ghost story. ISBN 0-930044-79-7   7.95

HOME IN YOUR HANDS by Lee Lynch. 240 pp. More stories
from the author of *Old Dyke Tales*. ISBN 0-930044-80-0   7.95

EACH HAND A MAP by Anita Skeen. 112 pp. Real-life poems
that touch us all. ISBN 0-930044-82-7   6.95

SURPLUS by Sylvia Stevenson. 342 pp. A classic early Lesbian
novel. ISBN 0-930044-78-9   7.95

PEMBROKE PARK by Michelle Martin. 256 pp. Derring-do
and daring romance in Regency England. ISBN 0-930044-77-0   7.95

THE LONG TRAIL by Penny Hayes. 248 pp. Vivid adventures
of two women in love in the old west. ISBN 0-930044-76-2   8.95

HORIZON OF THE HEART by Shelley Smith. 192 pp. Hot
romance in summertime New England. ISBN 0-930044-75-4   7.95

AN EMERGENCE OF GREEN by Katherine V. Forrest. 288
pp. Powerful novel of sexual discovery. ISBN 0-930044-69-X   8.95

THE LESBIAN PERIODICALS INDEX edited by Claire
Potter. 432 pp. Author & subject index. ISBN 0-930044-74-6   29.95

DESERT OF THE HEART by Jane Rule. 224 pp. A classic;
basis for the movie *Desert Hearts*. ISBN 0-930044-73-8   7.95

SPRING FORWARD/FALL BACK by Sheila Ortiz Taylor.
288 pp. Literary novel of timeless love. ISBN 0-930044-70-3   7.95

FOR KEEPS by Elisabeth Nonas. 144 pp. Contemporary novel
about losing and finding love.   ISBN 0-930044-71-1   7.95

TORCHLIGHT TO VALHALLA by Gale Wilhelm. 128 pp.
Classic novel by a great Lesbian writer.   ISBN 0-930044-68-1   7.95

LESBIAN NUNS: BREAKING SILENCE edited by Rosemary
Curb and Nancy Manahan. 432 pp. Unprecedented autobiographies
of religious life.   ISBN 0-930044-62-2   9.95

THE SWASHBUCKLER by Lee Lynch. 288 pp. Colorful novel
set in Greenwich Village in the sixties.   ISBN 0-930044-66-5   8.95

MISFORTUNE'S FRIEND by Sarah Aldridge. 320 pp. Histori-
cal Lesbian novel set on two continents.   ISBN 0-930044-67-3   7.95

A STUDIO OF ONE'S OWN by Ann Stokes. Edited by
Dolores Klaich. 128 pp. Autobiography.   ISBN 0-930044-64-9   7.95

SEX VARIANT WOMEN IN LITERATURE by Jeannette
Howard Foster. 448 pp. Literary history.   ISBN 0-930044-65-7   8.95

A HOT-EYED MODERATE by Jane Rule. 252 pp. Hard-hitting
essays on gay life; writing; art.   ISBN 0-930044-57-6   7.95

INLAND PASSAGE AND OTHER STORIES by Jane Rule.
288 pp. Wide-ranging new collection.   ISBN 0-930044-56-8   7.95

WE TOO ARE DRIFTING by Gale Wilhelm. 128 pp. Timeless
Lesbian novel, a masterpiece.   ISBN 0-930044-61-4   6.95

AMATEUR CITY by Katherine V. Forrest. 224 pp. A Kate
Delafield mystery. First in a series.   ISBN 0-930044-55-X   7.95

THE SOPHIE HOROWITZ STORY by Sarah Schulman. 176
pp. Engaging novel of madcap intrigue.   ISBN 0-930044-54-1   7.95

THE BURNTON WIDOWS by Vickie P. McConnell. 272 pp. A
Nyla Wade mystery, second in the series.   ISBN 0-930044-52-5   7.95

OLD DYKE TALES by Lee Lynch. 224 pp. Extraordinary
stories of our diverse Lesbian lives.   ISBN 0-930044-51-7   8.95

DAUGHTERS OF A CORAL DAWN by Katherine V. Forrest.
240 pp. Novel set in a Lesbian new world.   ISBN 0-930044-50-9   7.95

THE PRICE OF SALT by Claire Morgan. 288 pp. A milestone
novel, a beloved classic.   ISBN 0-930044-49-5   8.95

AGAINST THE SEASON by Jane Rule. 224 pp. Luminous,
complex novel of interrelationships.   ISBN 0-930044-48-7   8.95

LOVERS IN THE PRESENT AFTERNOON by Kathleen
Fleming. 288 pp. A novel about recovery and growth.
ISBN 0-930044-46-0   8.95

TOOTHPICK HOUSE by Lee Lynch. 264 pp. Love between
two Lesbians of different classes.   ISBN 0-930044-45-2   7.95

MADAME AURORA by Sarah Aldridge. 256 pp. Historical
novel featuring a charismatic "seer."   ISBN 0-930044-44-4   7.95

CURIOUS WINE by Katherine V. Forrest. 176 pp. Passionate
Lesbian love story, a best-seller. ISBN 0-930044-43-6 8.95

BLACK LESBIAN IN WHITE AMERICA by Anita Cornwell.
141 pp. Stories, essays, autobiography. ISBN 0-930044-41-X 7.50

CONTRACT WITH THE WORLD by Jane Rule. 340 pp.
Powerful, panoramic novel of gay life. ISBN 0-930044-28-2 7.95

YANTRAS OF WOMANLOVE by Tee A. Corinne. 64 pp.
Photos by noted Lesbian photographer. ISBN 0-930044-30-4 6.95

MRS. PORTER'S LETTER by Vicki P. McConnell. 224 pp.
The first Nyla Wade mystery. ISBN 0-930044-29-0 7.95

TO THE CLEVELAND STATION by Carol Anne Douglas.
192 pp. Interracial Lesbian love story. ISBN 0-930044-27-4 6.95

THE NESTING PLACE by Sarah Aldridge. 224 pp. A
three-woman triangle—love conquers all! ISBN 0-930044-26-6 7.95

THIS IS NOT FOR YOU by Jane Rule. 284 pp. A letter to a
beloved is also an intricate novel. ISBN 0-930044-25-8 8.95

FAULTLINE by Sheila Ortiz Taylor. 140 pp. Warm, funny,
literate story of a startling family. ISBN 0-930044-24-X 6.95

THE LESBIAN IN LITERATURE by Barbara Grier. 3d ed.
Foreword by Maida Tilchen. 240 pp. Comprehensive bibliography.
Literary ratings; rare photos. ISBN 0-930044-23-1 7.95

ANNA'S COUNTRY by Elizabeth Lang. 208 pp. A woman
finds her Lesbian identity. ISBN 0-930044-19-3 6.95

PRISM by Valerie Taylor. 158 pp. A love affair between two
women in their sixties. ISBN 0-930044-18-5 6.95

BLACK LESBIANS: AN ANNOTATED BIBLIOGRAPHY
compiled by J. R. Roberts. Foreword by Barbara Smith. 112 pp.
Award-winning bibliography. ISBN 0-930044-21-5 5.95

THE MARQUISE AND THE NOVICE by Victoria Ramstetter.
108 pp. A Lesbian Gothic novel. ISBN 0-930044-16-9 4.95

OUTLANDER by Jane Rule. 207 pp. Short stories and essays
by one of our finest writers. ISBN 0-930044-17-7 8.95

ALL TRUE LOVERS by Sarah Aldridge. 292 pp. Romantic
novel set in the 1930s and 1940s. ISBN 0-930044-10-X 7.95

A WOMAN APPEARED TO ME by Renee Vivien. 65 pp. A
classic; translated by Jeannette H. Foster. ISBN 0-930044-06-1 5.00

CYTHEREA'S BREATH by Sarah Aldridge. 240 pp. Romantic
novel about women's entrance into medicine.
ISBN 0-930044-02-9 6.95

TOTTIE by Sarah Aldridge. 181 pp. Lesbian romance in the
turmoil of the sixties. ISBN 0-930044-01-0 6.95

THE LATECOMER by Sarah Aldridge. 107 pp. A delicate love
story.   ISBN 0-930044-00-2   5.00
ODD GIRL OUT by Ann Bannon.   ISBN 0-930044-83-5   5.95
I AM A WOMAN by Ann Bannon.   ISBN 0-930044-84-3   5.95
WOMEN IN THE SHADOWS by Ann Bannon.
                                            ISBN 0-930044-85-1   5.95
JOURNEY TO A WOMAN by Ann Bannon.
                                            ISBN 0-930044-86-X   5.95
BEEBO BRINKER by Ann Bannon.   ISBN 0-930044-87-8   5.95
    Legendary novels written in the fifties and sixties,
        set in the gay mecca of Greenwich Village.

VOLUTE BOOKS

JOURNEY TO FULFILLMENT   Early classics by Valerie   3.95

A WORLD WITHOUT MEN   Taylor: The Erika Frohmann   3.95

RETURN TO LESBOS   series.   3.95

These are just a few of the many Naiad Press titles — we are the oldest and
largest lesbian/feminist publishing company in the world. Please request a
complete catalog. We offer personal service; we encourage and welcome
direct mail orders from individuals who have limited access to bookstores
carrying our publications.